Is That All There Is . . . ?

Is That All There Is . . . ?

Jane Tierney

Marionette Books

© Jane Tierney 1998

First published in 1998 by
Marionette Books
1 Hutton Close
South Church
Bishop Auckland
Durham

British Library Cataloguing in Publication Data.
A Catalogue record for this book is available
from the British Library.

ISBN 1 84039 007 7

Typeset by CBS, Felixstowe, Suffolk
Printed and bound by Antony Rowe, Chippenham

DEDICATION

To Sir Dirk Bogarde, our finest film actor and novelist

PART ONE

ONE

Jenny Sankey's first disillusion happened when she was six years old. She had been taken by her Mother to a pantomime. The excitement of the outing had begun when she first woke up that Winter's morning. She could hardly be bothered to eat any breakfast or any lunch. Then it was time to get ready to walk to catch the bus. Her Mother didn't drive. It seemed a long way to the town but, once there, she had danced along the pavement clutching her Mother's hand.

The theatre was huge and the foyer crowded. Her Mother had tickets for seats in the dress circle, and they climbed the stairs, all red-carpeted, into a vast place all garlanded with swags of red and gold velvet and lit by hundreds of light bulbs. Cherubs looked down upon them from the ceiling and a girl in black with a white frill round her neck and a white apron sold them a programme. Their seats were central in the second row and Jenny gazed in wonder at the great stage. There was a brilliantly coloured curtain showing nymphs and shepherds dancing in a clearing in a wood.

Jenny stared and stared. More lights were switched on and a band began to play. The figures on the curtain did not move. Tears began to well up in Jenny's eyes and began to roll down her cheeks. Her Mother bent over her and asked her what was the matter.

'Is that all there is?' Jenny quietly sobbed.

'No, no, silly girl. That's just the fire curtain. It will go up soon and the pantomime will start.'

After a few minutes all the lights dimmed, the band played more softly and the curtain rose. The stage was full of painted people. Dick Whittington was a grown up lady with big fat thighs and his cat was a man wearing a shabby pretend cat-coat. Loud songs and tap dancing, then they all started to sing. A clown with a fly-swatter kept hitting people, then a very thin

3

man tapped the fat-thighed lady on the shoulder and told him to go back to London. All the expected enchantment of Dick Whittington and his cat had gone. Jenny didn't understand. She had actually liked the fire-curtain better.

'We'll have an ice-cream in the interval,' her Mother said, but as it was a matinée there was no interval. 'I expect that's because there's another show at six-thirty!' Mother explained.

Jenny tried hard to understand what was happening on stage. She fiercely disliked the short fat girl in pink tulle with sausage curls, kissing the fat-thighed lady Dick. The man in the brown striped cat-suit looked nothing like a cat.

The curtain rose and fell several times and then everybody clapped and it was time to go home.

On the bus Jenny cried again. She said, 'Our Tigger could have acted the cat. We could have lended him.'

Tigger was a big neutered tabby with a green collar to match his eyes.

Her Mother spoke sharply to her, calling her a baby, and Jenny wet her knickers. When they reached home there was a real scolding and she was sent to bed without any supper.

Her next great disappointment came while they were staying at their rented holiday cottage in North Wales. Her Father, who painted in water-colour, said she could go with him to see the dawn come up over the mountains. At Llanbeddr at four-thirty in the morning it was very cold and damp, but Jenny, who loved her Father very much, kept still and quiet, watched and waited. At first it was barely possible to see the jar of water, brushes and paint box, but soon the colour of the sky changed and her Father told her to watch the sky and got busy splashing on watery streaks on a large pad. Over the mountains the grey did change to pale peach and he cried out, 'Look Jenny, those warm colours come from the sun, isn't it wonderful . . . ?'

Jenny wasn't at all sure what she expected but certainly something more exciting. She began to feel hungry and thought of breakfast down in the cottage.

The picture was nice and she was pleased her Father was happy. She busied herself emptying the water jar and wiping the sable brushes, then raced off down the hill glad to be feeling warmer.

4

She had two brothers older than herself. She adored Alan, the elder by eight years, and from the beginning he had a great influence on her life. From the age of seven onwards he supervised her reading, took her for walks and told her a lot about plants, trees and animals. It was he who told her when he considered the time right about the facts of life. When she started bleeding at thirteen, thinking she was dying of some fatal illness, he explained gently but explicitly that she should be proud to have become a woman. Then he told her about procreation and birth and something of love. She wanted fervently to marry him. She had learned in school that in a certain period of ancient Egyptian history the Ptolemis believed in brother marrying sister, so why should she not marry Alan? He explained that this had proved not to be a good idea, but he remained her guide and mentor for many years.

Her early school was a local private one. The boys went to a nearby Grammar School. At twelve she was sent away to a famous girls' boarding school in Buckinghamshire. She hated the place from the start and ran away several times because she couldn't bear being separated from the boys. She would get lifts from lorry drivers who were always kind, often sharing their thick sandwiches with her and setting her down a mile or so from her home.

At fourteen she was expelled and her Mother decided that she should be sent to France to finish her education. She lodged with family friends of her Mother's and went to a daily Cours. She liked the life and took quickly to the language which she had started and enjoyed at her English school.

She was there for four years and passed her *Baccalauréat* quite successfully.

After school she wanted to stay on and become apprenticed to a couturier. She even succeeded in getting an interview with Maggy Rouff where, she was told, she would probably have to spend the first year picking up pins from the floor and making the coffee before getting into the *toiles* room, then two years there before learning to cut.

Her Mother's friends managed to get her tickets for some of the big dress shows and she became enthralled with the idea, but her parents would in no way agree to letting her live alone in Paris and her Father came to take her home. Her French by this time was fluent and she supposed her family thought she might do a teaching job in England.

Still closely influenced by Alan she continued with his reading lists and by this time had also read her way through a great number of the French classics.

Shortly after returning home her brother brought home a pretty girl he had met at university. Jenny felt venomous towards her, went up to her room and sulked.

She had made one close girlfriend in Paris – Nicole Bruneau, who could not understand why Jenny was not interested in boys. She herself had several boyfriends and taught Jenny a lot about sex.

Playing in her wealthy Mother's jacuzzi bath, Nicole taught Jenny to masturbate. She began to appreciate such sensations, but after two or three times felt only guilt and a deep sense of self-disgust and gave it up. She began to wonder if she were frigid as she didn't care for any of Nicole's young men.

By this time she had grown into a very attractive girl. The attraction lay largely in her colouring. She had very dark blue-black hair, a fair skin and enormous bright blue eyes. Her friend told her she had the habit of lowering her lids when talking to someone then raising them suddenly and giving the full blaze of her vivid blue eyes. Nicole said they were Siamese cat colour. Jenny was of medium height, slim with long legs and full breasts. Nicole thought she should be a model or try for the stage. Neither of these ideas appealed to Jenny one bit and she was more or less resigned to teaching.

One day her Father brought home a business friend called Myles Lander. Her Mother told her he was a wealthy lawyer. He was quite old but very distinguished-looking. Jenny found herself admiring his car. She had never seen an Aston Martin before. It must be great, she thought, to be able to afford anything you wanted in life.

When introduced, he held on to her hand seconds more than was usual and said hesitantly, 'You are remarkably beautiful, Jenny. I was not prepared for such—'. His voice tailed off and her Father laughed.

'You must not flatter her,' he said. 'We have had quite a lot of difficulty bringing up this girl.'

Jenny explained briefly about her years in Paris and how much she had wanted to follow a career in couture but was forbidden.

'Just as well,' Myles said. 'We would almost certainly have lost you to some French fellow.' While saying this he looked deeply into her face causing a faint flush to colour her cheeks.

Alone that night in her bed, she realised that one way of having and doing the things one wanted in life was to have money. Then she thought of Alan and knew he would despise her for thinking such thoughts.

The next morning she wrote him a long, fond letter explaining that she must seek a teaching job and asked his advice on how to go about it. By this time her brother was headmaster of a well-known public school and married to the girl he had brought home from Oxford.

After meeting this lovely girl Myles Lander drove home in a trance. He could not get the image of her out of his mind. That face haloed by the dense blue black hair and those amazing eyes – the full gentle mouth slightly crooked when she smiled. He was in the grip of an emotion he had not felt for a very long time. He felt hopelessly consumed with a need to impress her. She must have read his heart in his face. He was in the process of discovering the simple truth – that he was still capable of love. He wanted to know all about her. It had been a *coup de foudre*. He had fallen hopelessly, deeply in love with Jenny.

That evening he made an excuse to get in touch with her Father again concerning the sale of some woodland in Berkshire and suggested calling in to see him the following evening. The meeting was planned for six o'clock.

Meanwhile, Jenny had questioned her Father about their distinguished caller, and was told that he was a very rich and well-known lawyer. He had been married but his wife had died in child-birth a long time ago. The child was still-born. He not only made a great deal of money from his work, but had inherited a fortune from his Swiss mother. He had a flat in London and a big house at Beaconsfield.

The meeting between the two men was brief and Myles Lander only caught a glimpse of Jenny crossing the hall on the way to her room. Her Mother invited him to stay and have dinner but he excused himself on the pretext that he had to go to Italy early the following morning. However, he said that he would very much like to invite them all to lunch with him in London. Would Friday – in three day's time – be possible? Mrs Sankey was asked and said she would be delighted and she was sure Jenny would be pleased to come. It was agreed that they should meet at The Connaught at twelve-thirty.

He reached his car with a lighter step and looking up at the upstairs window thought he caught a glimpse of a dark head beside a curtain. He waved and a hand waved back.

Driving back to London he was aware that he was breaking the speed limit but felt twenty years younger and without a care in the world.

Meanwhile, in the Sankey ménage he was being freely discussed. On being told of their lunch invitation Jenny showed no particular pleasure but her Father knew she was impressed. Her parents agreed that Myles Lander was very smitten with the girl but he was much too old to be encouraged. It had all been too sudden for anything to be read into it. On the other hand, if the girl herself took a liking to this older man, James Sankey would do nothing to prevent their association. Lander was a fine and honourable man who might have just the right temperament to guide the rather difficult and head-strong girl.

Let matters take their course.

TWO

The lunch was memorable. At least, for Jenny it was. The hotel itself was so sumptuous in a restrained sort of way. There were fresh flowers in a low bowl on their table and the pink linen cloth and matching napkins delighted her. Myles was rather casually dressed in cavalry twill trousers and a brown suede jacket. Without asking what they would like to drink, he ordered champagne and they sipped from hollow-stemmed glasses. Jenny sat between him and her Mother and spent the first ten minutes translating the menu. The dishes sounded delicious but her Mother disappointingly ordered grapefruit and grilled sole. Jenny chose snails and *blanquette de veau*. She was pleased when Myles chose the same.

When the menus had been taken away and glasses refilled, Myles congratulated her on her French and asked her if she was interested in paintings. She replied with enthusiasm and told him about some of the lesser known galleries she frequented in Paris.

'I have a few interesting pictures you may care to see,' he told her. 'You must come over to Beaconsfield and see them one day if you would care to.'

She said she would very much like that and asked him if he had any of the Impressionists.

'Several, actually, and some moderns. How about tomorrow?'

'Thank you, I would like that,' she replied, then turned to her Mother and asked if that would be all right with her.

Her Mother rather quietly agreed to the suggestion, then the men embarked on a political discussion and Jenny was left to chat to her Mother about the excellence of the food. From time to time she stole a sideways glance at Myles and liked what she saw. His light brown hair had silver streaks at the temple and above the ears and his bony aquiline nose gave

9

him a very patrician profile. He had beautiful hands and used them effectively.

For dessert they all agreed to have *crêpes Suzette* which were flambéd at the side of the table and followed by excellent fresh coffee. The men ordered brandy but Jenny and her Mother declined liqueurs.

Her Father had parked his car at a meter in Berkeley Square so Myles walked with them to see them off.

They all thanked him profusely and he touched Jenny's arm and said, 'I'll pick you up at eleven-thirty tomorrow, if that's all right?'

She smiled and nodded her acceptance, and they drove off.

'Well, you've certainly made a conquest there!' her Father said as they reached Piccadilly.

Her Mother frowned and said, 'Don't encourage the girl. He is much too old for her. Let things take their course. He could be a very good friend for her to have and to help her find a suitable job.'

They were all silent for the rest of the journey home and Jenny went straight up to her room to hunt through her wardrobe for something suitable to wear for her outing the next day. She decided on a simple white shirt blouse, a straight white piqué skirt and navy blue blazer. She knew that finest navy nylons and dark blue court shoes flattered her long legs. She would borrow a navy purse she had seen her Mother use.

Meanwhile, downstairs, her parents were heavily into a serious discussion about this man's infatuation with their daughter. Infatuation it certainly was, they agreed, but she must be advised not to show her own feelings – just let the friendship take its course and one would see how it developed.

'How old did you say he is?' her Mother asked.

'Getting on for fifty, I think,' her Father answered.

'Then he's nearly thirty years older than Jenny – it's out of the question,' Helen Sankey said firmly.

'Don't bring up the subject in front of the girl. Let us just see how things develop,' her Father said soothingly. In his heart he knew full well that this man had fallen in love with his daughter and, as far as he was concerned, he couldn't think of a more honourable man to entrust her to.

When Jenny came downstairs she kissed her Mother fondly and said, 'I'll make dinner this evening. We don't want much after that super lunch do we?'

Surprised and pleased, her Mother agreed that an omelette would be more than adequate. 'No doubt you learned to make a good one while in France. Thank you darling. Get a lettuce from the garden and mix a vinaigrette.'

For the rest of that day none of them mentioned the man who was uppermost in all their minds and eventually Jenny said she was feeling tired, and went up to have a bath before going to bed early. Too excited about the next day to read, she went to sleep early and dreamed about Alan. If only he were here to talk to. She knew that if she rang him up his wife would answer and say he was busy as she always did. Jenny decided she would borrow the family car one day soon and go and see her brother. She dreamed about him but in her dream he was ill and she woke up at five wondering if it could be true.

At breakfast her Mother said she had had a cheerful letter from Alan saying he would be down to see them soon, and all her nightmare fears vanished, and she could look forward to her luncheon date with a clear mind.

At eleven-thirty on the dot, the Aston Martin swept into the drive and Jenny walked out to meet Myles. He was dressed much the same as the previous day except the suede jacket was replaced by a tweed one. They went into the house together to say hello, and then goodbye to her parents and soon were on their way to Beaconsfield. He drove carefully and he asked her about her time in France and what she felt she had gained from it.

'Fluent French for life,' she declared firmly, 'and a fair knowledge of food, wine and literature. And, of course, a very great love of Impressionist painting.'

'I go to Paris fairly frequently on business,' he said, 'but I don't know the place like you do. I would very much like you to show me some of the smaller galleries you mentioned. I shall be interested to see what you think of my humble collection. Actually there is a Matisse drawing coming up in Bonham's sale next week which I intend to bid for. Perhaps you would like to come with me? That sort of sale can be very exciting.'

'I would like that very much,' she answered, wondering if her parents would approve.

11

Shortly they were driving through Beaconsfield town and turning down a lane beyond. 'My place is called "Foresters" and I own the paddock and woods behind.'

'Why Foresters?' she asked.

'Because years ago, when the Earl of Exmouth owned most of this part of the country, his head forester used to live there. I have enlarged the place considerably and rather like the name,' he answered, as they swept into a drive through an avenue of trees and came to a large square Georgian house of rosy-orange brick with an imposing front door painted white.

Jenny could see that there was a glass structure on one side of the house and was told it was an Orangerie with self-heating and ventilating machinery built in. Myles grew tropical plants, small trees and hoped to start orchids soon.

'Ugh! I hate orchids,' Jenny said.

'Very well – no orchids then, but why the dislike?'

'I think there is something sinister and evil about them; they make me shudder and I don't find them beautiful.'

'But you will love my little lemon tree which has already two tiny lemons on it and my plumbago and bougainvillaea.'

'They sound lovely. I should love to see them,' she said as he opened her door of the car.

As they approached the front door, it opened suddenly to reveal a heavy middle-aged rosy cheeked woman who greeted them with a slight bow. Myles introduced her as Mrs Sproson his housekeeper and explained to her that Miss Sankey was a young friend who was interested in seeing his house.

'What time would you like lunch, sir?' Mrs Sproson asked.

'Oh – in about half an hour, I think. I'll ring,' he replied.

From the spacious hall which had a parquet floor and many priceless Persian rugs, Jenny was led into the dining room. This was high and vaulted with more polished parquet and big dark-red Bokhara rugs; Victorian style high-backed chairs, a long mahogany table and a vast empty fireplace. Jenny looked around for stags' heads but there were none. Three or four dark pre-Raphaelite paintings in heavy gilt frames hung on one wall and a row of etchings on another.

Back in the hall she noticed two staircases leading up to a gallery where she could see hanging many interesting pictures. She felt eager to see them. No doubt they were all originals. First a pale Matisse of a plump young naked woman reclining, a pale washed pink and green aquatint, and next to it a very different canvas of which Myles said he was sure she wouldn't know its origin. Jenny studied it for a few moments. The deep reds and brilliant greens could only be the hand of one man.

'It's an early Chagall,' she said firmly.

'My goodness, you obviously know your French schools,' Myles said, sounding very impressed.

Next came a green countryside Manet and then, to her surprise, a reproduction (behind non-reflective glass) of the Renoir – Girl reading – which was her favourite Renoir. She told him so and said what a pity he didn't have the original.

'That's either still in the Louvre or possibly in America, I'm afraid. Well out of my reach.'

Next came an early Picasso rather like the one of the girl in the Tate Gallery and finally a David Hockney. A blandly simple painting of a table and a chair with the sea beyond.

'While we are up here I will show you the first floor of the house, then we can go and see my water colours in the drawing-room.'

The main bedroom seemed vast with all the furniture under dust sheets. It was painted a rather sickly blue but had big windows looking out over the garden and, off it, a beautifully fitted bathroom. Going through that she came across a small room, quite obviously Myles' dressing room, and off that another small bathroom.

Crossing the landing he showed her two guest rooms, each with its own bathroom and, at the end of the landing, a small square room with a big desk, filing cabinets, a fax machine, revolving leather chair and a television set. Obviously his office. A row of Hogarth vulgar drawings, which didn't interest her, and some dowdy old green velvet curtains which did. This was obviously where he spent most of his time and she could, she felt, so easily make it attractive.

'Time for lunch, I think' he said. 'The upper floors are just store rooms but could so easily be converted into anything one wanted . . .'

Going back through the master bedroom he stopped near the door and dragged a dust sheet off a small table with a glass lid. Raising it, Jenny was delighted to see a collection of miniature enamel boxes. She had only recently started a collection of her own, she told him. So far she had only two.

'Then choose a third!' he begged her. She looked carefully and settled for a small heart-shaped one with blue flowers on the lid.

He picked it up and handed it to her. It was Bilston enamel and obviously very rare and costly. She held it carefully, then opened the lid. The inside was bright blue enamel and under the lid in gold were the words 'I love thee'. She blushed and lowered her lids and to her surprise he leaned over and touched his lips to her forehead.

In the full blaze of her blue eyes she said, 'Thank you, Myles. Thank you very much. It's the finest present I have ever been given.'

Going down to the dining room he explained that the Sprosons, Ethel, and also Ernie, who looked after the garden, had their own separate ground floor flat with their own furniture and telephone. They seemed comfortable and happy enough.

Lunch awaited them in the dining room, which was quite funereal in atmosphere, but the food excellent. A delicious water-cress soup, followed by tender roast beef with ratatouille and to finish, a light lemon souflée. With all this they drank a pleasant white wine nicely chilled. The coffee was strong and awful.

Jenny begged Myles to congratulate Mrs Sproson on her cooking, to which he replied, 'Come with me and praise her for yourself.'

She let herself be led through to a big old-fashioned kitchen where the housekeeper sat at a scrubbed top table thumbing through a recipe book.

The big woman got to her feet and took Jenny's compliments shyly and when asked how to make water-cress soup said, 'You must come here one day and I'll be glad to show you.' She was obviously pleased by the praise and suggested her Master should show his guest the garden.

They walked through a side door and Myles introduced her to Ernie who was weeding a splendid herb bed. 'You must come at asparagus time. We grow the best 'ere. 'Aint that right, sir?'

'It certainly is,' Myles replied and led Jenny on to admire the herbaceous borders and the vast lawns. Then the Orangerie.

Back in the house Myles said he was glad she approved of the Sprosons.

14

'They come from the North, surely,' she asked.

'Yes, indeed. But the North is not a place you come from, it's a place you leave.' he said with a grin.

Jenny was not amused. She did not like such cryptic remarks he was often guilty of making.

He asked her if she would like to go to the bathroom and indicated a small cloakroom just inside the front hall. She excused herself, washed her hands and smoothed her hair and added a touch more of her currently favourite scent then went quickly to rejoin him.

'Now I suppose I must take you home, or your parents will think I have kidnapped you,' he said laughingly.

'I must just see your drawing room,' she said shyly, and he took her hand and led her into a vast room off the other side of the hall. It appeared to be carpeted and furnished entirely in pale beige, the only colour being in cushions and lamp shades. The paintings were modern abstracts which didn't interest her and she told him so.

'Then I must educate you,' he whispered.

'No, I will stick to my Impressionists and a few of the Florentines,' she replied. 'I did a two year course on the Florentines.' He seemed impressed.

'Then you must take me to Rome and Florence and educate *me*,' he said humbly.

She collected her blazer and they walked out to the car. They drove quite a long way in companionable silence until they saw a lone magpie. 'Oh dear, slow down, we must see another one. It's the only superstition I have,' Jenny muttered.

He slowed their speed and a second one flew from a hedge.

'Great! Now all will be well,' she said sighing.

'What a sweet, funny girl you are,' he said fondly. 'Do you find me boring? Old and boring, I mean?' he asked seriously.

'Certainly not. You are the most interesting friend I have ever had.'

'Then will you come up to London with me next Thursday?'

'For what purpose?' she asked, having forgotten that he had already mentioned about a sale at Bonham's that following week.

'As I said, I believe there is a Matisse drawing on sale at Bonham's which I would like to bid for. It can be quite fun.'

Feeling annoyed with herself for forgetting about their previous

15

conversation, she said, 'Oh, yes. Sorry. You've already said. Yes, I would like that very much. Do you set yourself a limit on price at these auctions?'

'Not always,' he confessed.

The journey had passed so quickly they were suddenly turning into her home driveway.

'Come in and say hello to my Mother. She would appreciate that.'

'Certainly, then I must race up to town for a boring meeting.'

Her Mother was delighted to see them and asked Myles if he would stay for tea or a drink, but he explained he had a meeting but would like to take a rain-check on the invitation.

'I quite understand,' her Mother said. 'Well, thank Mr Lander and walk him out to his car, Jenny.'

She took his hand casually and as they reached his car he bent and kissed her lightly on her cheek. She put a hand on his shoulder and held him for a brief moment. He smelled of some sort of wood, or was it leather? Anyway, it was no ordinary cologne. She liked it.

He took both her hands in his and said, 'Could you ever care for me, Jenny? I have been so lonely for so long and have never met anyone I felt about as I feel about you.'

'I like you a lot,' Jenny said shyly. 'I can hardly bear to wait till next Thursday . . .'

'Then how about tomorrow? Can I come for you about two o'clock?'

'I'll be ready. Town or country?'

'Town,' he said firmly, and smiled mysteriously into her eyes.

She more or less pushed him into his car and waited while he turned before running back into the house.

Her Mother quizzed her about 'Foresters' but Jenny said little.

Up in her room she threw herself across the bed and tried to remember that faint lovely smell she had liked so much pressed against his shoulder. She liked it better than her own scent.

Then she began to think seriously about the man. He was obviously in love with her. He was so rich, if she married him she could have anything she wanted in life and she could make an end to his tragic loneliness.

What was the alternative? The idea of teaching in some small school was abysmal. She began to smile thinking of all the trips abroad they could make – the theatres they could frequent. To be mistress of the big house was a bit alarming but Mrs Sproson already seemed to like her. She would make alterations, improvements and she would make Myles happy. He usually looked so sad.

She stayed in her room until dusk when she heard her Father come home. They must be discussing her now downstairs.

She changed into a simple old dress and went down.

They had obviously been discussing her and Myles as they both stopped talking as soon as she entered the room.

'I think now is the time to tell you, Jenny, that Myles Lander has asked my permission to propose to you,' her Father said.

Her Mother immediately began voicing her own opinion, saying, 'I have told your Father that the whole idea is absurd. The man is at least thirty years older than you. You have had no experience of life yet. By the time you are a woman he will be an old, old man. I do not approve of the idea at all.'

'What about you Jenny, what do you think?' asked her Father.

'Of course I feel flattered. I like him a lot. We have several interests in common. I should be taken care of for the rest of my life. I think he is a good and charming man.'

'I feel I must tell you that he telephoned me in my office just before I left and asked if it was all right with me to take you to London tomorrow.'

'Good, for I have already accepted his invitation.'

Her mother then took her turn again. 'The whole idea is, I repeat, absurd. You must not rush headlong into this just because the man is rich and you could have anything you want. You should wait a while. Get to know each other properly, even become engaged if necessary, but marriage is so final. I am adamantly against the idea.'

Jenny went over and sat beside her Mother and showed her the tiny enamel box Myles had given her and said, 'I really am already a bit in love with him, you know, and he has been so sad and lonely for years. I would like to try to make up somehow for this. Besides, he is very fit for his age, which I gather is about fifty. What does age matter? I like older men!'

'Well, I know my views count for nothing,' her Mother continued. 'I suggest you ask Alan's opinion. You might listen to him.'

'All right. I'll ring him tonight,' Jenny replied with a smile on her lips.

THREE

Jenny was near her window pondering over what her brother had said the previous evening. He had said neither age nor money were to be considered between two people if there was a genuine respect and love. She did truly respect Myles. As for love, she felt a strong attraction to him. She would like him to kiss her, she would then know if her feelings were love.

She heard, then saw a car sweep up to the house, but it wasn't Myles. It was a rather sedate BMW, and a man in a peaked cap was driving. Then she saw Myles sitting beside him.

Hastily she smoothed her hair, checked in the mirror to see if her lipstick was right, seized her purse and bounded down the stairs.

Her Mother was not in the house so she ran out towards the car and greeted Myles. who looked very formal in a dark suit and vivid silk tie. Then she noticed that the man in the peaked cap was Ernie, who got out, touched his cap to her, and held open the rear door of the car for her, then whisking quickly to the other side to open the other door for Myles. Completely mystified she waited for Myles to explain.

'Don't look so alarmed' he said. 'We are going up to town and it's easier with a driver.' He brushed her cheek with his lips and said, 'It's not the great kidnap you are always half expecting. All will be made clear to you shortly.'

She sank back into the comfortable upholstery and relaxed. Myles said he was taking her to London for a special purpose but would she mind if they paused in Hyde Park?

'Not at all,' she answered. 'But why?'

He took one of her hands in his and said, 'I have a special fondness for the Serpentine and would like to see it once more with you.'

18

They did not speak again until they had turned off past the Science Museum and entered the park. He told Ernie to park just past the bridge and when the car stopped, he led her back to the bridge and they looked over at the water. He then turned her to face him with his hands on her shoulders and said slowly and solemnly, 'Jenny Sankey, will you marry me?'

She had been looking down but now she opened wide her big blue eyes and in a faint voice said, 'Yes.'

Suddenly there was tears in his honest, deep-brown eyes and he said, 'You have made me happier than I have ever been in my life,' and, putting both his strong arms around her, hugged her close then kissed her very gently on the lips. Pulling her back towards the car he muttered something to Ernie and helped Jenny into the back seat.

They circled the park and left it at Hyde Park Corner, went down Piccadilly and into Bond Street. They did not stop until they came to a smart jeweller's shop on the left. 'Come back for us in one hour, Ernie,' Myles said as he helped her out and opened the shop door.

The place was solemn as a church and an elderly man in a grey suit came forward to meet them. In a matter of seconds Jenny's eyes took in thousands of pounds worth of costly jewellery.

'Now, what kind of ring would you like, my darling?' he whispered.

'What for?' she asked gauchely.

'An engagement ring – the choice must be entirely yours. I rather hoped you would choose a diamond solitaire—'

'I don't really like diamonds, and I prefer silver to gold,' she answered firmly.

'Then it shall be platinum, which looks more like silver but is costlier than gold. How about a sapphire surrounded by diamonds?' he suggested.

They were steered towards two chairs and a younger man appeared with a velvet tray covered with sparkling gems. There was one in the very middle which caught her eye and imagination. A big oval sapphire of medium blue encircled with small square cut diamonds.

'You like that?' Myles asked gently. 'It's not so valuable as the darker stones.'

'It's the colour I like best, and it's set in the metal you mentioned which looks silvery.'

19

'Well, try it on.'

Jenny held out her left hand and the assistant put it on her third finger. The ring was too big.

'That's no problem. it can be reduced to your size in days,' Myles said, 'but wouldn't you like to see the solitaire diamonds?'

'No, I much prefer sapphires,' Jenny said quietly.

The assistant and Myles exchanged glances and then her finger was measured.

'While we are here, let us look at wedding rings,' Myles suggested. There was a tray of platinum rings close by, and Jenny picked one up. It was broad and had vertical grooves in a clever pattern. She tried it on, but the only finger it would fit was the first finger of her right hand. She held out her hand and Myles kissed it and said, 'Keep it on, at least until they can provide the right size. Keep it on to remind you of today.'

She laughed shyly and leaned against him. 'At least it will help break the ice at home – I mean,that your intentions are honourable.'

Myles produced a credit card and asked when the sapphire ring would be ready.

'Forty-eight hours, sir,' the man said.

'Then deliver it to my chambers,' he said, giving the man a business card.

They wandered round the shop looking at all kinds of jewels. Jenny did not dare voice any admiration in case Myles insisted on buying it. At last they both shook hands with the senior man and left the shop to find Ernie waiting for them.

On the way home Jenny felt deliriously happy and kept touching the heavy platinum ring on her index finger.

Myles put an arm round her and kissed her neck and her ear. Jenny shrank back wondering if she had washed her ears in the shower that morning. Myles thought it was because of the presence of Ernie, so did not persist.

'Must we go straight to your home, darling Jenny?' he asked.

'Let's do something I have always wanted to do,' she said. 'Have tea at the Ritz!'

'Of course, if that is what you would like,' he said, and told Ernie to drive them there and then park at the In and Out Club almost opposite.

The Ritz lived up exactly to her imaginings. Echoes of tea dances in the twenties were conjured up as they sat at a dainty table and were offered wafer-thin cucumber sandwiches and little iced cakes. A single rose in a slender glass delighted her and she laughed at Myles's obvious boredom. She drank several cups of tea and then went to the delightful powder room.

When she came back to him he insisted they go somewhere they could celebrate properly with champagne. She agreed and, when they went to find Ernie waiting duly for them outside, Myles directed him to one of his clubs.

Over her second glass of champagne Jenny said she felt she should ring her parents to let them know where she was and what time to expect her.

'Would you like to dine in town or go back to Foresters?' he asked.

'I'll ring first, and then Foresters,' she said, beginning to giggle in her excitement.

'Well, Ernie will be pleased, and Mrs Sproson is expecting me for dinner so we can certainly eat there.'

She found a telephone and spoke to her Mother telling her she was dining with Myles at Foresters and that she had some very special news. She rang off abruptly before any questions could be asked.

On their way back to the country she leaned her head on Myles' shoulder and inhaled the magic woody smell which reminded her of an old chest she had been allotted to keep her clothes in at the Paris flat. Cedar wood. That was it, cedar. She loved it and she truly loved him. She was the luckiest girl in the world and she would do her utmost to make him happy.

Mrs Sproson was delighted to see them, and when Myles told her their news she shook his hand and then held Jenny to her ample bosom and shed a few tears.

'I've made something special for dinner,' she said, and hurried off to the kitchen.

Alone at last, Myles took Jenny in his arms and kissed her slowly and lingeringly. She felt his tongue exploring her mouth and she responded and felt a mounting excitement overtake her. Myles withdrew first and, having installed her comfortably in the drawing room, went off to find more champagne and put it on ice.

21

For dinner they had filet steak en croute and tiny sliced green beans and a pineapple sorbet. Jenny was so excited she didn't eat very much but her eyes sparkled and she made Myles laugh doing a take-off of the rather grand man in the jewellery shop, then she kissed her big platinum ring and left her chair to kneel beside Myles and to say that she didn't deserve him.

He lifted her onto his lap and cradled her like a child and said it was he who was the lucky one. 'I can't wait to show you off to all my friends,' he exclaimed.

'That makes me feel like a horse!' she murmured.

'A beautiful thoroughbred,' he said, and poured her more champagne.

Over coffee, which she didn't care for, he wondered whether he should keep her to stay overnight but realised it better to see her safely back with her parents than give rise for any suspicion.

She dozed off all the way back, but had sobered up quite well when they arrived at her home and made their announcement.

FOUR

It was not until two days later when her Mother came rushing upstairs to show her the announcement in the *Telegraph* that Jenny really believed what had happened to her. Her Mother held the open paper before her and pointed to the 'Forthcoming Marriages' column and she read 'Mr Myles Lander C.B.E. and Miss Jennifer Sankey, etc., etc.,' that the full truth of her new status became clear.

'What does C.B.E. mean?' she asked.

'Commander of the British Empire, and soon no doubt he will be knighted,' her Mother said smiling and then laughing. 'Imagine yourself as Lady Lander!'

'How on earth did he get this into the paper so quickly, and why hasn't he telephoned?' she exclaimed. Within seconds the telephone bell rang and Jenny ran into her Mother's room to answer it.

Myles said, 'How are you this morning, my darling? So sorry I haven't been in touch but something urgent and important cropped up.'

'Where are you, Myles? I was beginning to wonder if you had changed your mind—'

'Darling Jenny, I'm in Paris in the Georges Cinq Hotel. I have one final meeting tomorrow morning and then I'll get a plane and come straight to you. Is that all right?'

'Yes, of course. I've missed you so much. I've just seen the *Telegraph* announcement. You didn't tell me you were so distinguished. I'll be waiting for you tomorrow afternoon.'

'I can hardly bear waiting to see you – I love you so much.'

'Darling Myles, I love you too. I'll hang up now and try to make some plans – about the wedding I mean. It's not going to be easy. My parents are very conventional.'

'Take care of yourself my love – until tomorrow then, goodbye.'

Her Mother, who had followed her into the room said, 'What do you mean – make plans for the wedding? We shall expect you to be engaged for several months before getting married.'

'Oh, we couldn't bear to wait that long. We are both so sure now, we want a very simple ceremony and then a long lovely honeymoon.'

Jenny flung herself across her Mother's bed and began singing a silly pop song.

'Oh, you are impossible. We must arrange a proper wedding with all our friends and relations present. Remember, it takes three weeks to get the banns read. Your father will see the Vicar for you no doubt.'

'Myles might prefer a Registry Office in town.'

'Then we would never forgive you, our only daughter—'

Her Mother sat down and began to cry. Jenny rushed over and put her arms around her and said, 'Of course I won't do anything to hurt you, but we can have a small simple ceremony in church and just a few people here afterwards.'

'Wait till your Father comes home. Then we'll discuss the matter thoroughly.' She blew her nose and dabbed her eyes and patted Jenny's head.

'If Myles is coming here tomorrow I must make a cake for tea,' she said.

'He doesn't eat cake.'

'How do you know?'

'We went to the Ritz, and he wouldn't touch anything there,' Jenny said and laughed, remembering Myles so ill at ease in the silly surroundings. 'He might stay for dinner, though. But don't prepare anything extravagant, he might have other plans.'

Jenny was right. He arrived just before three o'clock with Ernie driving the BMW. Having greeted Mrs Sankey he hastily explained that they would go up to Bond Street to collect the ring and come back for the evening.

In the car he could barely keep his hands off her and she felt her first real desire for him. Aware of Ernie they both sat up straight and held hands demurely.

The ring was ready and it fitted perfectly. Myles confirmed his order for the wedding ring to be made to match and they should, as previously arranged, send it to his chambers. The sapphire was brilliant and very beautiful. Tears sprang to her eyes as he placed it on her finger, saying, 'I'm so glad you don't paint your nails like some girls.' She was glad he didn't know that only a week ago her nails had been a bright coral pink. She would throw out all the bottles of coloured lacquer as soon as she had the chance.

Leaving London, they drove to Foresters where Myles parked his suitcase and briefcase and collected some mail. They then had a few words with Mrs Sproson before going to the garage for the Aston Martin and set off for Jenny's house.

She simply could not stop gazing at the lovely ring and he pulled a small velvet box from his pocket and handed it to her. Lifting the lid slowly she found another sapphire – this time a square stone of a slightly deeper shade set in diamonds and platinum to form a brooch. The box was labelled CARTIER. He insisted on pinning it on her plain white cashmere sweater and she found her compact to see the effect. It was perfect.

She nestled closer to him and kissed his cheek. At the next lay-by he stopped and took her in his arms and they kissed passionately for a long time. Jenny knew beyond any doubt that she would gladly let him make love to her as soon as it was possible. That woody smell again enchanted her and he was so handsome, what possible importance was their age difference?

At last they set off again and arrived at her home just behind her Father's car which had turned in at the gate.

Running into the house she could hardly wait to show off her ring and brooch to her parents. They were suitably impressed and a bottle of claret was produced and they stood in a small group toasting each other.

Myles explained his Paris visit to his future father-in-law and Jenny clung to her Mother with her ringed hand across her breasts.

After a long discussion about wedding plans, it was agreed that they should be married by their friend the Vicar in the local church. The banns should be read as soon as possible, and that only family and very close friends should be invited to be present and a small reception should be held at the bride's home. A one-time friend from her English school should be asked to be Jenny's only bridesmaid and Myles would ask his friend and partner to be his best man.

For dinner Mrs Sankey had made a simple but savoury shepherd's pie followed by fresh fruit salad, and at ten o'clock Jenny walked Myles out to his car. They embraced for a long time and Myles said he really must apply himself to two day's hard work if he was anticipating taking a longish period off for the honeymoon.

'Where will you take me, darling?' Jenny asked.

He replied, 'I would like it to be Rome then Florence, so we can both show off our splendid knowledge of the Arts.'

She said that sounded perfect, and reluctantly she let him go, begging to be telephoned soon. She said she would like to spend more time at Foresters and he was pleased to hear this.

After she had watched his car sweep out of the drive, she looked at the sky and vowed silently that she would be a good and unselfish wife to this man to whom she was now completely devoted. The stars seemed to twinkle back at her.

FIVE

Jenny and her Mother went shopping in Oxford for her wedding dress. In a small but exclusive shop near Christ Church they found a delightful outfit of slubbed off-white Chinese silk, a tunic top with short sleeves and simple straight skirt – the whole lined with very fine silk. The size ten fitted her as if designed specially, and the elegant saleswoman suggested a short simple veil held in place by a coronet of small white flowers with a touch of blue, all of which she was able to supply. With her Mother's perfectly matched pearls (her present to her daughter) and her sapphires, she looked enchantingly pretty as well as elegant. They then found some plain but expensive low-heeled white court shoes and gossamer flesh coloured stockings. Jenny felt contented that she was ready for her great day.

As they had already spent a great deal of money, she hardly dared ask for special underwear, but her Mother, quite reckless by now, agreed this was essential, so they found a department store and bought a filmy satin and lace bra and matching panties.

Jenny still had her Father's cheque to spend so she decided to use that for more underwear, nightgowns and a satin robe – another day in London, perhaps!

A few days later the opportunity for more London shopping arose when Myles was being driven up to London by Ernie. Jenny asked to be dropped off at Harrods and to be collected a couple of hours later.

There she indulged in satin nightgowns, one blue, one white and an elegant satin dressing gown with matching slippers. She only bought one new dress, a simple lightweight denim shirtwaister, suitable for wear on her honeymoon, and a plain small white handbag with a shoulder strap. Before she left the store she also bought several pairs of the finest nylon

27

stockings and a simple plain suspender belt.

Ernie drew up after she had waited near the main doors barely five minutes, and Myles stepped out to gather her and all her parcels up with obvious affection. They went straight to Foresters where Mrs Sproson regaled them with tea and wafer-thin sandwiches.

Alone at last they fell into each other's arms and Myles showered her with kisses and murmurings of adoration. He did not seem much interested in the details of the wedding itself, merely glad that it was to be soon and simple. He had already bought their air tickets to Rome and that was, for him, the most important detail.

After a while he stood up, straightened his jacket and took her for a walk round the garden, then into the Orangerie where he picked for her a small bunch of Plumbago flowers. She pinned them to the lapel of her white blouse and, when he looked at her, he thought he had never in his life seen such beauty.

Looking up at him the blaze of her eyes dimmed the harebell blue of the flowers into insignificance. He longed to show her off to all his business friends and their wives and reminded himself that very soon she would be his.

Jenny was quite anxious to get home to show her Mother her new purchases, so Myles went to the garage for his Aston Martin and quickly bundled her and all her packages into the car

He stayed to chat to her parents for a short time and then excused himself, saying he had so much work to deal with which he must clear up before the long honeymoon ahead.

When she went out to the car to see him off, he humbly said he would have to neglect her for a few days as he had another trip to Paris to fit in, and several difficult court cases pending.

Jenny was happy enough to accept all this, for she planned to do many things herself, all in some way connected with the great day ahead and simply said, 'Just ring me when you can. Don't worry about me, darling.' A final brush of his lips and she waved him off.

Inside the house her Father asked if she needed any more money for her trousseau, and she assured him that wouldn't be necessary. She had everything now that she needed. Her girlfriend bridesmaid insisted on paying for her own pale blue dress and, after several long telephone calls, it was agreed she should arrive the day before the ceremony and stay the nights before and after the wedding. A bouquet of white lilac and irises had been ordered for her and the colour of her hair ribbon agreed.

Mrs Sankey was happily busy deciding and ordering the food and drink for the reception, and also took on the task of ordering, writing out and sending the invitations. Myles had only given her the names of two male friends, only one of whom was married.

Her Father helped the jobbing gardener tidy up the drive and the flower beds and sent in his car for a special service.

When his wife insisted they hire a Rolls for Jenny and his drive to the church, he seemed a little hurt but agreed and arranged for a man from the garage to chauffeur his wife for the day.

Jenny was delighted that Alan would be coming. Her other brother was working in Canada and couldn't make the trip. It seemed sad to her that Myles virtually had no relatives except a half-sister called Sheena, married to a rich Greek and living in Cyprus. Jenny thought that some time she might persuade Myles to take her to the island. She had always been attracted by the place. All in good time, she told herself.

She had always worn her hair in a careless sort of bob, but decided to go to a really expert hairdresser to have it shaped and trimmed. She made an appointment and went up to London and returned with a beautifully shaped, slightly shorter bob with a half fringe falling over the right side of her forehead. Her hair shone and bounced and she was pleased but didn't dare tell her Mother how much the grooming had cost.

She next invested in a new pale rose lipstick and blusher and a good moisturiser lotion. She never used any make-up on her clear skin, but she begged a few more pounds from her Father to buy a small bottle of her favourite scent, reminding herself that bigger flacons could no doubt be bought cheaper at the airport duty-free shop.

With the cheque from her beloved brother Alan she bought two top-quality suitcases and a beauty-box, and had her new initials inscribed on each of them.

Various gifts began to arrive. Coffee pots, toast racks, place-mats and electrical kitchen gadgets. No one could possibly know that at Foresters all these things abounded. She told her Mother to keep any of them she needed.

Eventually the wedding day arrived, and after having tried on the white silk suit many times, she decided that it looked better when she didn't wear any panties, which created a line across her thighs and bottom. As long as her Mother didn't know she would go to church without any knickers.

The June day arrived and Jenny and her bridesmaid dressed nervously in Jenny's bedroom. Her friend's hyacinth-blue svelte dress complimented her own outfit perfectly and they smiled and hugged each other excitedly until called to go downstairs.

Alan was the first to greet her, and he told her she was very beautiful, which filled her with confidence. She clutched his hands and told Alan that he would like her husband-to-be and that she couldn't be happier. He kissed her carefully on the top of her head through the gossamer veil.

After a gentle touch of her Mother's hand she watched her bridesmaid and Mother and other members of the party go off in their cars. Then, ten minutes later the Rolls arrived and her Father carefully settled her into it. Her pretty bouquet of white flowers and tiny forget-me-nots smelled delightful, but above this she was aware of her own scent which she had used fairly lavishly because Myles had told her he liked it so much.

From then on she sailed through the ceremony at Myles' side, confident and deliriously happy and proud. Then the signing of the register and the return with Myles to her home, where everyone was vociferously awaiting them. She had never known such complete happiness.

The champagne was poured, and everyone began to relax. Myles introduced his best man, his partner Desmond Elliot, who made an eloquent and, in parts, funny speech.

Feeling more than a little intoxicated, she was told it was time to change into her going-away clothes. A simple white linen suit with a grey-blue blouse and white pill-box hat. Into the BMW with Ernie at the wheel, she tossed out her bouquet which fell straight into Mrs Sproson's arms. Looking embarrassed, the stout woman tossed it into the air and it was caught by a small girl from the village who had just come to gawp.

Sinking back at her husband's side he whispered, 'Now, Mrs Lander, you are all mine,' and squeezed her arm so tightly she almost cried out.

Aware of Ernie, she restrained herself and said, 'What about our luggage?'

'All taken care of, my darling, it's in the boot.'

Jenny closed her eyes and sank back and didn't speak again until they reached Heathrow.

A porter appeared instantly while Ernie was lifting their luggage from the boot. When he straightened up, on impulse Jenny kissed him on the cheek and thanked him, telling him to be sure and collect his wife from her house.

'Of course, Madam,' he said, 'and may you 'ave as many 'appy years as me and the missus.'

Before boarding the aircraft, she bought herself the promised scent in the duty-free shop. Then, almost as soon as they had boarded the plane, Myles ordered champagne. After half a glass, Jenny felt herself feeling pleasantly drowsy. Myles leaned over and settled her with her head on his shoulder and she didn't wake up until they were landing in Rome.

Quite suddenly she slid a hand down her skirt and realised that she hadn't any knickers on. She hadn't worn them with her wedding suit because of the line and the lovely satin briefs with lace edging must be still sitting on her bedroom chair. She hoped Myles wouldn't watch her undress and be shocked.

He asked her what was worrying her and she said she would tell him when she knew him better and giggled.

The Eden Hotel was magnificent. They saw their bags safely into their room and went down to the bar where Jenny begged for a cup of coffee. Myles had a brandy.

SIX

Before dinner Myles took her walking to the Trevi Fountain where they threw in coins and made their wishes.

Back at the hotel, after a brief tidying-up and washing of hands, they went down to dinner. The food was all new to Jenny, exciting and delicious. She refused to drink any wine, saying she had had far too much champagne for one day, and was feeling drowsy. They adjourned to a spacious sitting room and drank coffee and listened to a talented pianist playing gentle but moving pieces. Myles suggested that she might like to go up and prepare for bed while he went to the bar for a nightcap.

Jenny agreed at once, and Myles saw her into the lift. She undressed slowly, washed, sprayed on more of her precious perfume and slid into her white satin nightgown. The lovely blue satin robe she draped over a chair near the left side of the bed. She chose the left side because that was the side her Mother always slept on in the big double bed at home. Perhaps Myles would prefer another arrangement. She lay down in the lovely comfortable bed with a book upside down and feigned sleep. Soon she heard Myles coming in quietly and through her lashes watched him go into the bathroom and then on through another door. He must have ordered another room as a dressing room. A long time later, still pretending to read, she saw him come in wearing elegant dark blue silk pyjamas and slide into the other side of the bed. She opened her eyes, smiled at him and put down her novel on the bedside table.

Switching off her reading lamp she felt him moving towards her across the great expanse of bed. Very gently he slid one strap of her nightgown off her shoulder and began fondling her breasts. Then he leaned over her and kissed her neck, then her nipples lingeringly, and then her mouth. His was wet, and he forced her lips open and she felt his tongue searching her

32

mouth. She felt herself responding but experienced a sense of alarm when he began stroking her inner thighs.

To her horror she felt herself become moist and then an excitement took over and suddenly he was inside her pushing, hurting, so much so that she cried out – but she wanted him to go on. There was an urgency in her inner core which, in spite of the pain, silently begged him not to stop. He was moving frantically now and she was responding, her whole body reaching for a climax. Yes, yes, she silently begged – don't stop – go on and on – but there was a sudden explosion and she felt a wetness spreading between her thighs.

Myles had withdrawn from her and was lying limp and exhausted beside her muttering, 'My darling – my beautiful . . .' but he had turned away from her and was breathing heavily, then more deeply until she realised that he was asleep.

She wriggled and found some Kleenex tissues beneath her pillow and stuffed them into the dampness between her thighs. When her heartbeats had returned to normal, she dropped into a restless sleep. She woke suddenly about dawn and thought – is that all? and dozed off again, sleeping soundly.

The next thing she knew was seeing Myles in a dark-blue dressing gown ushering a maid with a loaded tray into the room, followed by a second girl bringing a similar tray. Myles took off his robe and got back into bed. She struggled to sit up and smooth her ruffled hair. Myles looked immaculate.

'My darling, did you sleep well?' he asked gently. 'Do you want to go to the bathroom before we have breakfast?'

'Yes, I think so,' she replied, managing to push the elegant tray towards the end of the bed and pull down her nightie, holding the tissues tightly between her legs. She shuffled into the bathroom and there she washed on the bidet, and was alarmed to see blood on the tissues (it wasn't her time for a period). She smoothed down her hair, which was defiantly curling up at the ends, went to the toilet, and washed her face.

When she returned to the bedroom, Myles was standing up beside her side of the bed holding her tray. She smiled at him and slipped beneath the covers, sat up and let him put the tray across her knees.

33

'My precious love,' he said 'how are you? Did I hurt you last night?'
'No. It was wonderful. I'm afraid I am not very good but I shall learn.'
'You were perfect, my darling,' he insisted. 'Now eat your breakfast.'
On the tray was fresh orange juice, toast, butter and jam and, under a
silver cover, a little mound of scrambled eggs. The coffee was hot and
good and she added a little cream from a tiny silver jug.

They ate their breakfast in silence, then Myles asked her what she
would like to do.

'See some paintings, then sit on the Spanish steps,' she managed to
say between mouthfuls. She was suddenly enormously hungry and ate up
the contents of her tray like a schoolgirl.

'My lovely, funny, sweet girl,' he said. 'You obviously hardly ate
anything much yesterday.'

'I ate that super dinner,' she reminded him.

'Well, you are very slim and I love to see you eat. I'll get out of your
way and use the bathroom, then you can take as long as you like to get
ready. I adore your curly hair!'

'It's not supposed to be curly! I like it straight. I shall have to dampen
it down and turn the ends under.'

'You are ravishing whatever you do, my love,' he said, getting out of
bed and depositing his tray on the floor. 'I shall wait for you in the big
foyer downstairs. It seems like a warm sunny day.'

After Myles had finished in the bathroom and had left the room, Jenny
pushed her tray to the end of the bed and got up, slipped off her nightgown
and went straight into the shower. When she had dried off in an enormous
bath towel, she took a brush to her hair and brushed it vigorously, turning
and pressing the damp ends into her smooth bob and forward on the
cheeks. She was no longer bleeding and put on first her pretty lace-edged
panties. Stupid me, she thought, for she had to take them off again to put
on her suspender belt and a new pair of nylons. Bra, half slip then the
pale blue shirtwaist dress and her sapphire brooch. A dab of moisturising
cream, a combing of her black arched eyebrows and a touch of rose lipstick,
a spray of scent and she was ready.

Myles rose to meet her in the great wide hall and, with a hand under
her elbow, they left the hotel.

To reach the galleries they had to walk down a narrow street full of fascinating shops. Jenny thought it the Bond Street of Rome. The shoe shops had the most beautiful, elegant shoes she had ever seen and there were belts and bags and scarves such as she had never seen before. Myles suggested that when they had seen enough of pictures she may like to come back to the street and do some shopping.

'What a generous husband you are, darling Myles!' she said, squeezing his forearm.

They went first to see the early Florentines. Jenny found the Giottos perplexing and Mantegna's foreshortening of the body of Christ was disappointing, but was overwhelmed by the magnificence of the da Vincis and the Boticellis.

After about an hour, Myles suggested they should rest a while over a cup of coffee. They went to the Via Veneto and sat at a pavement café and watched the world go by. Some of the Italian women were so ravishingly smart, Jenny was delighted when Myles suggested she may like to go shopping.

They found their way back to the narrow street and, within an hour, Jenny had chosen black patent leather shoes, a matching belt and handbag, several lovely scarves and six pairs of fine kid gloves. Myles would not allow her to carry any parcels for at each shop, after he had paid, he ordered them to be sent round to the hotel. Jenny felt like royalty.

She then pleaded with him to sit for a few minutes on the Spanish steps and soon it was time for lunch, for which they returned to the Via Veneto and ate the most delectable pasta dishes washed down with a mild sparkling white wine.

Taking a taxi back to the hotel they were both contented to retire to their room for a rest. That is, Myles reclined on a chaise-longue at the foot of the bed while Jenny unwrapped all her new possessions which had been delivered to their room. She insisted on trying every single item on and paraded in front of her husband who congratulated her on her good taste. It was true, her simple blue shirtdress was much improved by the black patent belt and shoes.

'Tomorrow,' Myles said, 'after we have seen another gallery we will buy you some dresses.'

'But darling Myles, you mustn't over-spoil me. I have already enough to get by on.'

'Then come and say thank you before you stuff all your goodies away.'

She knelt beside him and exuberantly showered kisses on his face and hands.

'Just lie beside me quietly for a little while,' he begged and she squeezed onto the couch close against his slim body and put her arms round his neck. 'You smell enchanting, my darling little girl,' he whispered in her ear, 'and I am the luckiest man in the world. You have given me a whole new life.'

They both drifted off to sleep and when they woke up it was almost five o'clock. They got up, yawned and stretched, and Myles ordered tea to be sent up. The tray arrived within minutes, brought in by yet another pretty waitress.

The tea, Jenny thought, was not very good, but the cream pastry she indulged in was. 'I shall get very fat and you won't like me any more,' she pouted, but he laughed at her and fondled her breasts through her crumpled dress.

'I shall now go down in search of newspapers my darling,' he said. 'I suggest you start getting ready for the evening. Have you a suitable dress to wear for dinner? I seem to have wrecked the one you are wearing.'

'I thought of putting on my wedding outfit with my sapphires,' she said.

'Lovely, darling. Tomorrow we'll go and buy you lots more pretty things.'

Jenny sat for a long time in front of her dressing-table mirror and spoke sharply to herself about not being greedy and extravagant and reminding herself to write a postcard home. She dampened her hair again and since Myles had said he liked it curly she brushed the ends upwards and out, forming the blue-black halo which Myles had first admired.

When she went downstairs she could not find Myles anywhere, but after a few minutes he appeared out of the lift dressed in a formal dark suit with a stripy green tie. He explained to her puzzled glance that he had a separate entrance to his dressing room upstairs. Was there no end to his extravagance, she wondered?

He told her they would dine early and go and see a play he had been told not to miss. It turned out to be a French farce by Feydeau which she already knew well and she was very touched and was able to whisper

36

translations of bits he might have missed. So, he was not only rich, extravagant and generous to a fault, but capable of gratitude too. She loved him more and more although dreading the love-making ahead.

It all happened exactly as the first time, except she grew more deeply excited and cried out for him not to stop. She never reached her climax and she began to wonder if she ever would. Perhaps she could ask an older woman about such matters, or buy a sex book.

Every night they were in Rome the same thwarting bed palaver took place. It must be her fault, she decided firmly, for Myles was a man of the world and obviously had made love to more than one woman. She would have to sort the problem out somehow – if she could.

SEVEN

On their fourth night, frustrated and puzzled, Jenny could not get off to sleep so went and lay down in a warm scented bath and pondered the situation. She could hear Myles snoring.

During the last two days, after viewing more world-famous paintings, they had spent a lot of time buying Jenny a collection of the most elegant and beautiful designer clothes for both day and evening wear. Then they had to buy another suitcase to contain them before moving on to Florence.

She was enchanted by the ancient city. They stayed in a big old-fashioned but very comfortable hotel near the Bridge of Sighs and spent many days in the famous art galleries where some of the well-known Italian masters' works seemed more eloquent and vivid than those in Rome. By chance they happened upon a small Goya which she knew and loved, and Myles said one day he would take her to the Prado to see the finest of this artist's works. Jenny already knew a little Spanish and decided she must brush it up before that holiday happened.

In the jewellery shops Myles insisted on buying her lapis lazuli necklaces and ear rings, insisting that she should wear lots of blue stones which were always out-dazzled by the blue of her eyes. In other shops they bought small leather goods to take home for presents for her family and the Sprosons.

They dined each evening in a different restaurant and Jenny always tried to remember the different herbs used in each especially wholesome dish.

All too soon after Myles had been in touch with his partner, he announced they must return home shortly as difficult cases were mounting up which he alone could cope with.

It was hard to believe that they had been away for over three weeks.

Jenny's cheeks and arms were lightly bronzed by the sun. She looked a picture of health in spite of her agonising nights.

On the flight home she experienced a sort of tingling feeling in her breasts, and felt a sort of lassitude. Both these symptoms were more intense during the first few days back at Foresters.

She consulted her diary and found that her period was overdue and one morning she felt quite sick. Was it possible that in so short a time she could be pregnant, she wondered? A visit to her old family friend and doctor embarrassed her but seemed the only solution. She gave a sample of her urine and three days later Doctor Graham telephoned her to say that one rabbit and she were pregnant.

That evening when she told Myles he was ecstatically happy with the news, and said he was sure it would be a boy. Looking at all those beautiful paintings was the finest thing she could have done in her early stages. He rang Hugh Graham himself for his opinion and was reassured to be told that his wife was in excellent health and there should be no complications. The right diet, healthy walks and contentment were all she needed and the doctor was sure all these things would be taken care of.

Mrs Sproson was delighted too with the news of the expected baby and found for Jenny a local dressmaker to make her some smart smocks for when she grew bigger.

On one occasion when Myles was out of the country on business, Jenny went for a trip to London and she bought lengths of lovely Liberty print materials for her maternity clothes and a plain skirt with an expandable waist.

Next she set to work having the nicest of the guest bedrooms and bathroom turned into nurseries. She kept the walls and woodwork all white, had a more modern suite installed in the bathroom, all cupboards lined with sweet smelling lining paper and left the choice of drapes and lampshades until after the child was born. She had found an interior decorator who said she could have any drapes and lampshades supplied within twenty-four hours.

After further consultation with the doctor, a bed was booked for her confinement and at Myles' insistence a qualified nurse was engaged for the first month of the baby's life.

Although Jenny protested that the latter was totally unnecessary, for she wanted to look after the baby herself, Myles was adamant. A less highly qualified nanny could be taken on after that period, Myles implied, but a nanny they must have so that Jenny was always free to be with her husband whenever an occasion demanded it or for acting as hostess at dinner parties.

From the time it was certain that she was pregnant Myles slept in his dressing room and treated her as if she were made of porcelain. This infuriated Jenny who, once past the sick stage, had never felt healthier or more strong in her life.

Myles certainly liked showing her off to his friends and clients and it was true, she had a sort of special bloom about her skin, her eyes were even brighter and she came in for lavish congratulations and compliments all round.

When she had finished adapting the rooms for day and night nurseries she found time on her hands and asked Myles to introduce her to a leading publisher. Somewhat mystified he did as she begged and she was given an appointment to go up to town to meet him. She felt herself capable of being a publisher's reader and after a longish conversation with the chosen publisher and a number of testing questions, was taken on.

Manuscripts began to arrive and Jenny thoroughly enjoyed reading them and returning them with remarks and criticism. Shortly she was offered more money to do some editing. This irritated Myles, but since she never neglected anything to do with running his house, she refused to be overruled.

Watching Mrs Sproson slowing up, she told Myles they should employ a daily cleaning woman for the house and leave Mrs S to her excellent cooking. Myles agreed gladly and Jenny soon found someone suitable in the village. Mrs Sproson was very touched and grateful for her concern.

So, the months passed, Jenny bloomed and swelled, developed a liking for anchovies and peppermints, but disliked alcohol and most sweet things.

Her labour pains started twenty-four hours before the doctor's estimated date and Myles, anxious and nervous, took her in his own car to the Nursing Home. She spent seven hours in labour and at midnight gave birth, naturally, to a fine strong healthy boy. Myles did not wish to witness the birth but waited till everything was tidied up and a rather tired Jenny was propped up in bed holding the baby in her arms.

He knelt by the bed and told her how clever and wonderful she was and kissed her hand, thanking her for giving him a son.

The baby opened his eyes and Myles exclaimed, 'He has your blue eyes.'

Jenny replied, 'All babies are born with blue eyes; his may change later to your shade of brown.'

Within two weeks of returning home the child's eyes were definitely brown.

The qualified nurse was efficient and strict. Nothing was allowed to interfere with the time-table she had decreed for mother and child. Jenny had a good supply of milk and was delighted to feed her baby herself. Myles would have preferred to engage a wet-nurse until assured by the doctor that Jenny's figure would be restored quicker if she followed nature's way.

She loved the experience of suckling the baby, feeling that he would always be close to her because of this, as indeed he was.

He grew rapidly. After the strict nurse left, Myles called an agency which supplied them with a cheerful, fully trained Irish girl called Bridie who Jenny took to at once. Life was not so regimented and stifling and the house became full of laughter and all too soon the baby, who had been christened Jonathan Myles, grew apace and bore a distinct likeness to his Father. Myles was delighted.

He did not return to the marital bed until the baby was weaned and no lovemaking was attempted.

After several nights of this, Jenny asked him what was wrong and stroked him gently and lovingly. Unfortunately, his attempts to enter her proved impossible and he apologised and slid down limply beside her.

'I don't know what is the matter with me,' he murmured. 'I shall have to consult a specialist. Forgive me my darling, for I love you so very much.'

The following week he stayed up in his town flat for three nights and Jenny imagined that during this time consultations with a doctor were taking place.

The first night home he slept in his dressing room and, when he did return to their bed, apart from fondling her, made no attempt at love-making. Jenny was puzzled but also somehow relieved.

41

At last, one evening over a glass of sherry he confessed to her that he had become impotent. She felt compassion for him but realised that what in her own mind she thought of as 'the bed palaver' was mercifully over. She would always be loyal to him and show her affection so that he would never experience shame over his condition. The only thing that worried her was that it seemed unlikely there would be any more children.

Myles became more and more protective of her and continued to bring her wonderful little gifts, but she was distressed by the fact that although he adored their child, he would never pick Jonathan up or even touch or fondle him.

When they went away on holiday to the South of France or to Italy she watched the French and especially the Italians kissing and cuddling their sons unashamedly, and so wished he would show some physical affection to Jonna, as she had started to call their child. She herself loved to hug and kiss the little boy and he returned her affection. Myles frowned on this and remarked she overdid her affection. The boy must be brought up to be obedient and to respect his parents.

By the time Jonna was four, Myles expected him to shake hands and to address his Father as 'Sir!' This made both Bridie and herself giggle, but they had to hold their mirth until Myles was out of the room.

If she hadn't had her editing to do, she would have gone mad, she thought.

She had made few friends locally and only one close one. She met her by chance in a nearby supermarket, they had introduced themselves as neighbours.

Lulu Gomez was a very tall attractive redhead who had once been a show girl then a model. She had a striking face, elegant legs and dressed in an avant-garde manner. She had been married several times and had a shy teenage daughter called Filly.

At the moment of their meeting, Lulu Gomez was trying to buy a lavatory brush. The sales girl said, 'You mean a toilet brush, madam?'

'No,' shouted Lulu adamantly, 'I don't want to brush my hair – I want to clean a lavatory with it!'

'Sh-sh – we call them toilet brushes, madam.'

'Damn silly,' remarked Lulu, who was standing near Jenny, and Jenny laughingly agreed.

They found themselves together again at the check-out and Lulu said, 'You, I believe, live at Foresters. I'm in the next patch along the lane. When you have put your stuff in the car, come and follow me home and we'll have a drink and get to know each other.'

Jenny gladly agreed. After putting her shopping into the small Fiat Myles had bought for her, she followed her new-found friend in her old flaming red Ferrari out of the town towards the lane to Foresters and beyond.

The drive to her neighbour's house was full of pot-holes. Through screens of conifers, Jenny glimpsed a lake and a tennis court, then the house itself came into view.

It was built in a conventional chalet style but much larger than average. The overhanging eves were painted a bright orange shade making it look like an advertisement for a holiday leaflet. Various television masts and a satellite dish were mounted on the roof. Jenny reversed her car alongside her new friend's vast machine. The front door was open and a voice called her to come in.

The chalet consisted of one enormous open-plan living space with a wide staircase leading up to a gallery which ran around three sides of it. Huge bold abstract paintings hung on the walls. There was a mass of hi-fi equipment in one corner and the biggest television screen she had ever seen.

Lulu stood behind a massive bar saying, 'What would you like to drink?'

'Whatever you are having,' Jenny said.

'I usually have a long cold vodka-tonic about now. Would that suit you?' Lulu said, already pouring.

'Great. Sounds good,' Jenny replied. She had never tasted vodka in her life.

Bringing over their glasses to a low sofa, they sat down and after offering Jenny a cigarette, lit one herself.

'I am between husbands right now,' she announced, kicking off her smart boots. 'I have caught sight of yours several times. Very distingué, but we have never met.'

'Then you must come over for dinner one evening when Myles is home,' Jenny suggested. 'Have you any children?'

'One son aged twenty-two studying in America. He is from my second

43

husband, an Argentinean, as is my very different convent-reared daughter Filly, aged sixteen. Her father being a polo player. I couldn't resist it!'

'I have just one son too, almost six now, but no doubt he will be sent off to prep school by the time he's seven. Myles is very strict with Jonna.'

'My Filly is due home shortly. She's very shy, obviously convent-reared and into poetry and the arts. May I bring her?'

'Of course. We have some interesting paintings she might care to see.'

'I feel sure your husband will approve of her, in spite of her brash Mother.'

'He loves meeting people.'

'I doubt if he will approve of me,' Lulu warned.

'Let me know as soon as Filly comes home and I'll fix an evening,' Jenny said.

Looking at Lulu closely, she noticed a lot of make-up and, on her fingers, a mass of diamond rings.

Before Jenny had taken a second sip of her drink, Lulu had emptied her glass and was on her way to get a refill. When she sat down again, Jenny asked her if she knew a lot of local people. They laughingly agreed that apart from the Vicar and the Doctor they knew no one.

'Myles is a barrister – he works in London and goes abroad a lot. We entertain many of his clients and lawyer friends. I do editing for a publisher, so one way and another I don't have much spare time,' Jenny explained.

'My God, you must be a real blue-stocking. I can't spell or add up and am practically illiterate,' Lulu confessed.

'Have you lived here long?' Jenny ventured to ask.

'No – months only. Before my last divorce I lived for years in the States, but since I am English and was born and bred here, I decided to come back. Filly has now gotten it into her head she wants to learn dressage – at least, seems to be keen to sit on a horse while it walks backwards on its hind legs!'

'Then she must be keen and it's a healthy enough activity. I have never tried it myself.'

'Well, my current lover is English and a polo player. He is over in the Argentine buying ponies now. We expect to be married quite soon. I don't seem to be able to get away from the gee-gees!'

Looking at her watch Jenny jumped up saying she must hurry home as her cook was waiting for various foodstuffs that she had bought.

'My! that's very grand, having a cook I mean. Fortunately I rather like cooking. You must both come to me soon and try me.'

Lulu walked her out to her car, giving her a card with her name and telephone number on it.

Jenny drove off feeling quite exhilarated by meeting this rather colourful new character with the lively personality but had grave misgivings about Myles' opinions on meeting the redhead.

To her surprise, when the event took place, Myles seemed quite captivated. He matched some of her slightly outrageous stories with some equally blue ones of his own.

By contrast, Filly proved to be a slight, shy girl with long fine pale red hair and a lisp.

At the return dinner, Lulu had cooked a very hot spicy Mexican dish and as a sweet a delicate mango sorbet. Her wine was excellent. When Lulu said her fiancé was due in a few days Myles insisted they should come over again as soon as possible.

Before this, however, Filly telephoned Jenny one morning asking if she could come and seek her advice over a problem. Surprised but flattered, Jenny named a time that same day.

Filly wanted quite simply for Jenny to explain to her the puzzling question of sex.

'But why me? Why not ask your Mother?' Jenny asked.

'Oh, Mummy's hopeless,' she replied.

'But surely you have been reading outspoken novels and such—'

'I just read one by Judith Krantz,' Filly said.

'Well, I can tell you, Judith Krantz it ain't. It's a messy, smelly, rather tiresome procedure; it often hurts, sometimes quite painfully. It's often disappointing. First of all, never never go to bed with a man unless you love him very much – then you can forgive anything.'

'What about multiple orgasms?'

'That's an expression used lavishly by writers like Jackie Collins but doesn't happen much in real life. I hope you will find out that I am wrong. My advice is always take a book and plenty of Kleenex tissues to bed with you.'

'But what about the actual act?'

45

'The man, if he has a hard penis, pushes it inside you and gets very aroused. It takes much longer for a woman to reach this state and sometimes he explodes inside you when you long for him to go on pushing. It takes much longer for a woman to become aroused. You may be lucky. Have you a nice young man interested?'

'Yes, but although he is keen I don't feel ready to jump into bed with him.'

'Then don't. Make him wait until you are so aroused and excited there is a chance it might be wonderful. You obviously know all about condoms and such?'

'Yes, we did all that at school but the actual act was never explained. You have been marvellous explaining and I am so grateful to you. You see, I don't want to be like my Mother and have lots of marriages and divorces. She has been engaged so many times too. You know, she has a box full of gorgeous stones. When she broke off an engagement she always sent the ring back and kept the stone.'

Jenny shrieked with laughter, finding this hilarious. 'Come and see me whenever you want to talk,' Jenny told the shy girl. 'I'll do anything I can to help you.'

After the girl had gone she laughed at herself and went to find Jonathan who was busy with a hammer, some nails and a piece of wood in the potting shed.

Jonathan quickly pulled an old sack over his pieces of wood. 'You mustn't look. It's a secret,' he said, rather red in the face.

'Sorry darling. I'll go away and get on with my own work.'

Kissing him on top of his brown head she hurried away, grinning to herself at the attempt at mystery. Perhaps he was trying to make a hutch or something to keep a small animal in. He had already made it known that he very much wanted a live pet and Myles had refused to allow this.

Jenny was aware that her son and her work were her salvation. This fact seemed to irritate Myles who, in a curious way, was beginning to treat her like a small child. He had developed the habit of abbreviating words – biscuits were now 'bickies', if she read late at night he would say 'time for beddy-bies' or 'it's nearly midders'. Drinks were 'drinky-poohs.' At times she wondered if his mind was going. He had certainly developed a slight paunch which aged his good looks and had slowed up his movements.

One dreadful day Ernie died of a heart-attack – in the asparagus bed – before they could get him into an ambulance. Jenny comforted Mrs Sproson as well as she was able, and asked if she wanted to go away for a while to stay with relatives after the funeral, but the poor woman said she had no living relatives she cared about and would rather continue working.

Myles ordered a headstone of Mrs Sproson's choice for the grave in the local cemetery and arranged for a daily man from the village to take on the gardening.

Mrs Sproson one day asked Jenny if she might have a puppy to lessen the loneliness. Jenny agreed without consulting Myles. She drove her friend up to the Battersea Dogs' Home and they chose a brown terrier type puppy, about six months old. He had already been house-trained, which made the project easier. When he looked up at her with his lion-coloured eyes Mrs Sproson was sure he was the one she wanted. She had bought and lined a basket for him to sleep in and it was good to see the woman smile again.

Jonathan was overjoyed and abandoned his construction of a rabbit hutch. Myles was livid and spoke angry words to Jenny who refused to be intimidated by him and said he would change his mind when he saw the difference it had made to his loyal housekeeper. She was right and Ben, as Mrs S christened him, became a family friend.

At the risk of making Myles even angrier Jenny answered an entry in the local paper and bought a three-months'-old Siamese kitten. Its training, using first a litter tray, then having a cat-flap built into the back door, proved simple, and the pair of animals put new life into the household. They were a constant cabaret and gradually Myles accepted them.

He was, however, very angry when naughty little Ming, instead of using his scratching post, started to sharpen claws on the back of a handsome brocade chair which had come from his Mother's house in Geneva. Jenny tried turning its back to the wall but the cunning little cat would squeeze in behind and still manage to rip the brocade to shreds.

After a couple of drinks one evening, Myles pulled the chair out and looking at it closely, to Jenny's surprise began to laugh.

'The problem is – we don't know whether to brush it or comb it!' he said, smiling. She was astonished at this good humour and wondered

47

what he would have to say if he knew that on nights he was away, she let Ming sleep on her bed.

She and Mrs Sproson both delighted in the animals' antics. Sometimes the dog would pretend to maul the cat and had to be pulled off, but a few seconds later the cat would prance with arched back in front of him, asking to be chased.

One day the young cat took Ben's bone up a tree and the frantic dog barked loudly and pawed the ground until the bone fell down. Ben had already been neutered and Jenny had to take the young Siamese down to the vet for the same operation. Ming quickly recovered and the animals' normal behaviour resumed.

Jonathan loved them and they loved him. What he dreaded most about going away to school was being parted from them.

EIGHT

The summer before he was due to go to his prep school they went on holiday to the South of France. They stayed, as usual, at the Negresco in Nice and on Myles' insistence took Bridie with them. Jenny pointed out that this was unnecessary for a boy of almost eight, but Myles said they must be able to go out to dinner sometimes further along the coast, and it was essential that someone should be left to take care of the boy.

Jenny longed to go in search of wilder beaches, unspoilt villages in Haute Provence or even round the corner into Italy, but Myles was contented enough with the Promenade des Anglais and the private beach with its orderly rows of deck chairs provided by the Negresco. The only alternative being the similar private beach provided by the Carlton at Cannes. They stayed at the Carlton on alternate years so were always welcome to use the hotel's beach.

Myles was very proud of his wife's excellent French and, when they visited the Picasso Museum in Nice, he listened with amazement at her fluency when discussing the artist's work with the curator. He determined to try to buy another Picasso, preferably from his early period, whenever he found the opportunity. He himself did not like any of this artist's work, but he wanted very much to please and surprise Jenny with such a gift.

It was while they were looking at paintings one day he decided he must have her portrait painted. After many enquiries he commissioned Anna Alexeiva, a Russian artist.

So for the whole month Jenny had to go up to the artist's studio near the Tower of London, three times a week.

The studio, which was vast, had once been a dock warehouse and Anna positioned Jenny against a brick wall and made her wear a simple denim shirt which drew attention to the brilliance of her eyes and would

49

not date. Myles would have liked to see his beautiful wife in full evening splendour but agreed to the artist's decision.

As she painted, Anna talked of her own life's experiences and kept Jenny fascinated and motionless, listening spell-bound to the woman's colourful adventures.

When she was finally allowed to look at the portrait of herself she saw at once a likeness had been definitely achieved. Myles would be very pleased and, when they both drove up to collect the canvas, they insisted they take Anna out to dinner.

It was a warm and entertaining meal and they drank a lot of champagne so Myles, after dropping off the artist and paying her, suggested they should spend the night at his small flat instead of risking his breaking the law on his way driving home. This was the first time Jenny had seen his small flat in the Albany and was amazed at its old-fashioned, if somewhat restricting, charm. Jenny slept on the single bed and Myles on a couch.

The next morning they dropped the painting off at the picture framer's in St James's and drove home for an early lunch.

Myles brought home the framed portrait triumphantly a few days later. Mrs Sproson and Jonathan were bidden to admire it. Mrs Sproson said she should have worn one of her lovely evening gowns, an opinion with which Myles agreed, and Jonathan said she looked as if she was in prison. However, they all agreed it was a good likeness, and Myles then set about finding the right position in which to hang it. After many unsatisfactory positions he settled for over the Adams fireplace in the drawing room. Jenny much preferred a painting of a tiger which she had picked up at a local auction sale, but no one else liked it so she hung it in her own little work room on the second floor.

All too soon the day arrived when it was time to pack for Jonathan's entry to his prep school. Sewing on of the labels was done with the help of Mrs Sproson at the kitchen table, and soon the small cabin trunk, cases and tuck-box were all ready. Jenny was glad when Myles offered to take the boy, for she knew she would be bound to shed tears on leaving Jonna. As soon as she had seen her husband and son off, she drove over to Lulu's and had several drinks and stayed to an impromptu lunch of smoked salmon and Camembert cheese, and giggled to Lulu's account of her latest flirtation with a minor film star.

The house seemed horribly empty when she got back to Foresters, and she sought Mrs Sproson's company until Myles got back.

To her surprise, Myles came in in high spirits and said he would like to take her away for a holiday. 'Istanbul!' he declared triumphantly. 'A place I have always wanted to go to and never had the time. I have the name of a small French hotel there. You would like that, wouldn't you, my darling?'

'Sounds interesting, but could we not go on to Cyprus and see your half-sister, it's not so far from there, is it?'

'No. I can't stand her fat greasy husband, and I think it's a boring island.'

'All right, then Istanbul it is. Should be quite warm there still. I must pack some light clothes.'

'I have booked flights for Thursday, that's in three day's time.'

'I'll be ready,' Jenny said.

The flight by Turkish Airways left a lot to be desired and the passengers all clapped after the somewhat bumpy landing.

The hotel, situated very near all the mosques, turned out to be rather twee with lots of reproduction Louis XVI furniture and brass bedsteads, but the food was French and good, and there was a pleasant garden at the back with lots of cats and kittens to keep Jenny happy feeding them scraps from her plate.

On the first morning, Myles suggested visiting some of the mosques and the Topkapi, but Jenny only wanted to see the latter. She had previously seen a film about it and was fascinated by the biggest diamond in the world.

Myles went off alone to see the Blue Mosque while Jenny unpacked, and then came back to collect her. Jenny had expected the place to be warm but it was cool and very dusty, and there were far too many museums and mosques.

At the Topkapi, guide book in hand, Myles would stand for a long time in front of each object or artefact they encountered. Sometimes he would stare for so long at one object that Jenny believed he was doing it to test her patience. She was sure his doctor would not have approved of his standing about for so long.

Having seen the fabulous diamond, she couldn't wait to get out into

51

the fresh air, but he refused to be hurried. She was sickened by the smell of feet. When at last he had had his fill she suggested they go and sit at a pavement café and have a drink. Better still, she said, would be to take a taxi up the hill to the Hilton, from where they would get the best view of the Bosphorus. Myles reluctantly agreed.

The view was splendid, the drinks were well chilled and politely served, and she began to feel better tempered.

Myles suggested that the next day they might venture into the Bazaar or Souk which was reputed to be the biggest in the world.

So, the next day, once inside the souk they found themselves surrounded by clamouring merchants – even plucking at their arms and clothing and small boys running behind chanting 'Ze Englees 'ave short arms and long pockets!'

They pressed on deeper, and Myles bought her a pale grey leather coat which was elegant but smelled rather strongly, and some ropes of rough hewn dark turquoise beads. For Mrs Sproson they bought an ornate deep shopping basket.

While they were paying for this, Jenny noticed a well-dressed American woman who was staying in their quaint hotel. She was buying slender gold bracelets, even though she already had so many on her arm that when she raised it to pat her hair, there was a tinkling, chiming sound as they softly crashed to her elbow.

They then bought some toys, miniature cars and animals which Jenny thought much too juvenile for their son.

Gazing East, Jenny asked again about hopping over to Cyprus, but was abruptly silenced. Myles lapsed into a bad-tempered mood which lasted for the rest of the day.

They spent the rest of their time there buying some small patterned rugs which Myles said resembled closely his own Persian ones. He wanted to give them to his partner for his next birthday. Desmond Elliot was not well-off enough to buy luxuries, Myles informed her.

Jenny was relieved to be home again – to see Mrs Sproson and the animals, and two manuscripts from her publisher to be edited.

A few days later Myles went again to visit his doctor, but even after starting on a new set of ampoules, his sexual prowess was no better and he at last became resigned to his state, apologising once more to Jenny who assured him it made no difference to her feelings for him. This was not strictly true, and at various dinners and parties she found herself occasionally admiring another man without making her feelings obvious.

The months and the years sped by. In the school holidays Jonna was as fond and affectionate as ever to her, and loved their goodnight chats when he would stroke her hair and beg her to stay and chat to him. But later, when he went to Harrow in his early teens he had a crush on a young English Literature master and the caresses ceased.

He had grown taller than his Father and was bright academically and a good games player.

PART TWO

NINE

The year is 1972. Jonathan has been a great disappointment to his Father. He went up to Oxford to Christ Church, his father's college, to read Law,but after one year declared he was not making any headway, never intended to practice it,and wanted to change to studying foreign languages.

He took French and German and then an extra year for Spanish. When this was completed he asked to be sent to the Harvard Business School for one year. Myles grudgingly financed this.

To Jenny's surprise and Myles' dismay, there he met an attractive American girl called Gayle and they married before they both graduated. He got a good job in banking in New York and was posted to London, where he was placed in an even better position.

At first, they lived in a small flat but after their first child was born, they moved to a house in Barnes. Soon afterwards a second child arrived so that at forty-two, Jenny was a grandmother to a boy and a girl.

The boy was rather delicate, with pale red hair and a shy manner and the girl, unsuitably called Fleur, was thick-set with dark hair and eyes like two blackcurrants. Whereas Timothy was timid and easy to cope with, Fleur was loud, demanding and greedy.

Myles, who had aged visibly and now wore glasses and rarely drove himself, disapproved of the young household so they did not meet on many family occasions. Jenny saw them quite often at their place in Barnes, and took a great interest in the children's prowess. She didn't invite them often to Foresters, fearful of Myles' displeasure.

One evening, Jonna telephoned to say Gayle had a special favour to ask and, when he put her on the line, Gayle explained that she very much wanted to go and see an old school friend who had married an Englishman and lived near Bath. As she would be away for two nights she asked Jenny if she could go over and stay in Barnes to look after her grandchildren while she was away. A bit apprehensive, Jenny agreed and they fixed a time and day.

Myles was quite scathing about this, but Jenny determined to do this small task.

She set off quite early one morning before Myles was up and, with the help of a road map, found her way easily enough to the house in Barnes. She parked behind her daughter-in-law's car and went into the house. Gayle was already dressed for the journey and had a case in the hall beside her. The children came running downstairs and Jenny bent and kissed them in turn. Timmy was shy and quiet, but Fleur began crying and clinging to her Mother's coat.

She sobbed, 'I want to go with you – I don't want to stay with Grannie.'

'Nonsense – you'll help Grannie, show her where everything is, won't you?'

'I don't like Grannie,' Fleur gulped, rubbing knuckles into her eyes.

Timmy caught hold of her and said, 'Come on, we'll show Grannie the house and where everything is.'

'Bloody Grannie – I hate her,' the child screamed.

'Please take no notice of her. It's her new word,' Gayle said. 'I've left a shepherds pie in the fridge and there are plenty of tins of fruit in the cupboard and cream in the fridge. Soup and baked beans on toast for their supper. Chops and spinach for you and Jonathan tonight.

The two women brushed cheeks briefly and Gayle picked up her case and skipped out of the front door, slamming it behind her. They heard her revving the engine of her car and driving off.

Timmy took Jenny's hand in his, grabbed his howling sister with his other, and led them into the kitchen.

'Bloody Grannie,' the small girl repeated, yet stopped crying instantly.

After taking off her coat, Jenny was led to read the notice board in the kitchen. All emergency numbers were written at the top. Then below, the fact that Fleur wouldn't drink milk unless it had chocolate in it.

Timmy showed her his latest designs, while scowling Fleur sucked her thumb. The little boy drew surprisingly well. He liked dressing dolls and his Mother had bought him pieces of brightly coloured felt to work with.

He could cut out and sew together small trousers or a dress and pin them on to a soft fabric stockinette covered doll quite expertly. Perhaps he was a budding Yves St Laurent, Jenny thought and was amazed at his cleverness.

Fleur had now stopped crying and was trying to draw Jenny's attention to herself.

'I could help you make a pudding!' she announced loudly. 'I know how to make pastry. We could have a treacle tart.'

'Well – I hadn't thought of making pastry,' Jenny said. 'Wouldn't you rather have junket and fruit?'

'I hate bloody junket!' Fleur said, stamping her feet.

'Shut up, Fatty,' Tim said, and told her to be polite to her grandmother or he would tell Daddy.

More cascades of tears followed but, ignoring these and talking to the gentle Timmy, made the little girl resort to another ploy.

'We could turn out the toy cupboard and throw out our old togs for the jumble sale. Come on upstairs,' she shouted and, seizing one of Jenny's hands, dragged her up to the first floor play-room. She tugged at the door of a big cupboard in the wall and a mass of toys, coloured bricks, stuffed animals and broken objects fell out.

'Oh bother! I don't feel like sorting this stupid bloody mess out!' she announced and flounced off leaving Jenny to push the whole mass back in again.

Downstairs, Timmy was pinning on a pair of sailor's trousers. Fleur was banging her fists on the other end of the table and saying, 'I'm thirsty, I want a chocolate drink.'

'Wouldn't you both like some nice orange juice?' Jenny asked hopefully.

'No, I hate bloody orange juice,' the fat child shouted, and continued banging her fists on the table.

Jenny began searching the cupboards for drinking chocolate. She found it and a jar of Nescafé. Meanwhile, Timmy had put the kettle on to boil. Jenny made two mugs of chocolate and one of Nescafé for herself. The children both helped themselves to spoonfuls of sugar and Timmy poured in milk. The greedy Fleur helped herself to four or five spoons of sugar until Jenny said, 'That's more than enough. You are too fat already. Do you want to be a monster?'

59

'Yes, I'll be a monster if I want to.'

Jenny took the sugar bowl out of reach.

'Now we can make the pastry,' Fleur announced when Timmy had put the dirty mugs in the dishwasher.

'Very well,' Jenny agreed reluctantly, and the process of finding the ingredients, the mixing, the spillages, the cleaning up and finally the putting of the tart and several grubby shapes cut out by the wilful child into the oven took them up to lunch time.

Hastily, Jenny put in the shepherds pie too, and made a note of the time.

Lunch passed without incident. Timmy told her about his school and how he liked drawing best. Fleur went to sleep with her head on the table.

'She usually has a sleep about now,' Timmy said.

Jenny sponged two sets of sticky fingers, then carried the podgy little girl up to her own room. She laid her on her bed and pulled the duvet up to her chin and tucked a teddy bear in beside her. In sleep she looked quite angelic, but by the time everything had been cleared up downstairs, Fleur was boisterously awake again. A walk was suggested but it had begun to rain turning into a downpour. The children agreed to play 'snap'.

After much shouting, tears and squabbling, they suddenly heard the front door open and Jonathan appeared. Jenny was much relieved to see her son.

'Hello, Mum. Have they been wearing you out?' he asked, kissing her affectionately.

'More or less,' she admitted.

Jonna suggested she should go upstairs and take a rest and said he would bring her a cup of tea later. He showed her into the guest room and quietly closed the door. Jenny sank down exhausted.

It seemed no time at all before Jonna was beside her with a cup of tea and Timmy wriggled up beside her whispering, 'I'm sorry old Fatty is so naughty. Thank you for looking after us.'

For the first time Jenny felt a surge of love for the small boy. In time, perhaps, the awful Fleur would grow more like him. Possible but unlikely, she reflected.

Jonathan, after reading the children a story, helped Jenny bath them and give them supper in their pyjamas, then put them to bed. She quite enjoyed making dinner for her son and he opened a bottle of wine and told her something about his job. He had a certain likeness to Myles, but in character was more like herself, Jenny thought. She was a little concerned that his hair seemed to be thinning on the crown of his head. He would all too soon have a bald patch. She suspected he was somewhat hen-pecked, for Gayle had a firm and direct manner.

They sat pleasantly at the table sipping the last of the wine until Jenny suddenly remembered that she hadn't made the beds. She excused herself and ran upstairs and went into her son's room and straightened out the bottom sheet of the vast double bed, smoothed the pillows and put the duvet on neatly. After picking up a few garments from the floor she put them into a wardrobe and went to inspect the adjoining bathroom. Here there were only towels to be placed on a heated rail and a washbasin to be wiped clean with somebody's face flannel.

Downstairs she found Jonna had cleared the table and had made a fresh pot of coffee. He placed it on a tray and led her into the comfortable sitting room.

They discussed Myles and his state of health. Jonathan said he thought his Father should retire and Jenny agreed.

'The trouble is, he would be so bored,' she said. 'It's a pity he never took up golf like most men of his age.'

Her son agreed, but pointed out that he was a great reader, and had his hobby of tropical plants for the Orangerie.

'I rather think I am guilty of spoiling his enthusiasm over that,' she confessed. 'You know, years ago he wanted to start a collection of orchids, but I told him I hated them, so he never did.'

'But there are still hundreds of other plant species he could cultivate,' Jonathan said, and Jenny agreed and felt some of her guilt expunged.

'I shall go to some specialist nursery and find out some names, and once he gets interested, he might well settle for that as a worthwhile occupation.'

The next day was much the same as the first with a few tantrums, a few spillages, a walk on the common and an ice-cream bribe to keep Fleur silent.

Jonathan stayed home the following day, and Gayle reappeared at tea-time so Jenny was blissfully released.

She found Myles already at home and, after washing her hands, she spent a blissful hour being cuddled on the big sofa and told how much she had been missed, then regaled with an excellent dry martini before dinner.

Myles told her that he had to go sometime fairly soon to visit a millionaire recluse who lived at Eze in Provence. His partner would go with him. They would stay in Nice and hire a car to go up into the hills.

Jenny sometimes missed her own Mother. Her Father had died suddenly after a massive heart attack whilst gardening, and after the funeral her Mother had decided to go and live near her younger son in Canada. Jenny missed her Father very much but was not so stricken as when her older brother, by then Headmaster of one of the country's famous schools, died of lung cancer.

Some time after hearing this news, her Mother had died too. This left Myles and herself bereft of relatives and, because of this, closer together. Jenny still wished Myles would relent on the idea of visiting his half-sister in Kyrenia. She tried persuasion yet again, but without result.

TEN

The day after Myles had left with Desmond Elliot on the trip to Eze, Jenny had spent the day with Lulu and her new husband. They had taught her to play backgammon, and she had caught on very quickly and enjoyed the experience. Some good food had been consumed and a great deal of alcohol. Jenny felt distinctly dizzy driving the short distance home and went up to bed with Ming and a V.S. Pritchet novel, which she was reading for the second time.

At almost midnight the telephone beside her bed shrilled and, answering it, she recognised the voice. It was Rory (she had never known his surname), a young Irish accountant who worked in Myles' firm. He sounded agitated and short of breath. He told her there had been an accident. Myles and Desmond Elliot were both dead.

At first she thought there must be some mistake, and asked Rory to repeat what he had said, this time more slowly. He did. He said exactly the same. Myles and Desmond had hired a car in Nice and were driving up to Eze on a narrow tortuous road when they had had to swerve to avoid an oncoming truck. They had hit a stone wall and the front of their car was completely smashed – the two men must have died instantaneously. The poor boy was almost hysterical.

Jenny was numbed. He went on to tell her she would have to come out to identify the body of her husband. He had already booked a flight for the next day and a room at the Negresco for several days. He gave her the Air France flight number and the time she must be at London Airport. She wrote it down on the pad meticulously, then went to the bathroom for a glass of water. Myles dead. It wasn't possible. It was a bad dream. But she had not been asleep. She must pull herself together and organise her journey.

Although it was late, she rang for Mrs Sproson and told her the dreadful news. Mrs Sproson folded Jenny to her bosom and held her for a moment very firmly.

When she released her she asked exactly what Jenny would like her to do. Jenny told her to get her a medium sized suitcase out of the store room and to be sure to call her at six the next morning. Just a cup of tea would be all she needed.

When the elderly woman went down for the case, Jenny tried to decide what to wear and what to take. Would there be a funeral? She hadn't anything black. It was September and still warm. She could travel in her cream linen suit and take a dark blue dress. Her ticket would be at the Air France desk at Heathrow. She could park her car in the garage opposite.

Looking at herself in the glass she saw her face flush then drain of all colour. Then she willed herself to think clearly and began picking out items from her wardrobe and drawers. Silk shirts, changes of underwear, stockings, shoes, a Panama hat, a pale handbag. She found with relief she had plenty of money and, of course, her credit cards.

Mrs Sproson came up with the case and a small glass of brandy, and stood over her while she drank it. Then she started packing Jenny's things into the case.

At last all was ready. Jenny lay down on the bed and stared at the ceiling. Somehow the hours passed and at six Mrs Sproson came in with a tray of tea things.

She poured a cup for Jenny who sipped it slowly. 'Shall I telephone Master Jonathan?' Mrs Sproson asked.

'No, I will ring him myself from France when I know more,' Jenny said. 'I will, of course, ring you too. Just take care of Ming and Ben for me. I'll be all right.'

She dressed quickly and picked up her case and small overnight box which contained her make-up, wash things and a bit of jewellery.

By seven she was on the road and at eight arrived at the airport. Collecting her tickets from the Air France desk, she checked in her suitcase and went through to immigration and customs.

All went smoothly until after half an hour on the plane she began to sweat. The sleeves of her silk shirt were soon soaked. She had taken off her jacket which the stewardess had taken from her and hung up.

Presently, the girl reappeared and looking at her anxiously asked if there was anything she could get for her.

'Aspirins, if possible, please,' Jenny murmured.

The girl was quickly back with the tablets and a glass of iced water.

When the stewardess returned to take back the glass, she asked if anyone was meeting her at Nice airport.

'No,' Jenny replied, and then thought of the enormity of the fact. She would never be met again. This was real life. She had been cossetted, spoiled, sheltered for so long, she suddenly felt afraid.

As soon as they had landed and stopped taxiing, the kind stewardess escorted her first off the plane.

The heat was appalling. She climbed into the first taxi and said, *'Negresco s'il vous plaît,'* and they swiftly moved off.

I shall soon be seeing Myles, she told herself. Someone will come for me at the hotel – perhaps he is only injured – needing an operation, but soon she would be seeing him for herself.

Shortly after arriving at the room in her hotel, she was taking off her clammy clothes when the telephone rang. It was Rory. He was downstairs; he had come to take her to the mortuary where the bodies had been taken. The police had organised everything.

She quickly put on a clean shirt and a little scent, picked up her handbag and went downstairs. The place was so familiar – she had been here many times before. In the distance someone was playing a piano.

Rory looked dishevelled, older than she remembered him.

He said, 'If you don't feel up to it, I'm sure the police would take my word on the identification.'

'No, I want to go. I must see Myles for myself,' she insisted sharply.

She got into the hired car Rory was to drive. They drove through the town then began to climb on a winding road up towards Eze.

'He may be badly damaged. You will have to be very brave,' Rory said.

She did not answer.

At last they stopped at a grim looking barrack-like building which she supposed was a mortuary. There was a strange chemical smell in the air. With a hand under her elbow, Rory guided her inside. They went down some stairs into a basement. A man in dark green overalls led them to the far wall and pulled out a big drawer in the wall.

Under a sheet was Myles. He had a terrible wound on the side of his head. Part of his clothes had been cut away exposing a thin broken leg, an emaciated thigh, yet the expression on his face was peaceful as she had often seen it.

Rory nodded to the man who pushed the drawer back.

'Oh no!' she cried out, 'I want to see him – I want to stay with him.'

'I'm afraid that's not possible,' young Rory said firmly. 'There are papers to be signed. You are his next of kin. You must let me make all the arrangements for the funeral and burial.'

'Shall we take him back to England?' she asked.

'Not advisable. Better bury him here, as soon as possible. He loved this coast.'

'So soon?'

'The heat, you know.'

The thought of Myles' beautiful body being put into the ground made her feel sick and faint. 'I can't do it,' she said firmly.

They returned to the hotel, and Rory helped her up to her room and told her to lie down. He helped her stretch out on the vast opulent bed, and told her she did not have to do anything further. He would bring papers for her to sign; he would telephone Jonathan; he would arrange for the death notices to be put into *The Times* and the *Telegraph.* Then, in a couple of days, he would take her back to London.

Presently, the hotel doctor came to see her and gave her some sleeping pills. She took two and slept for about ten hours.

When she woke up she wondered momentarily if it had all been a nasty dream, but very quickly she knew the truth. She rang for some tea and toast and, after a bath, decided she should ring Jonathan. His line was busy. Half an hour later she tried again, but it was still engaged. Eventually she got through, and sadly discussed the terrible happenings over the last few hours.

She then took a long slow bath and waited for Rory. Eventually he came with the official papers for the burial.

She had to sign two papers, and he went away again but was back within an hour telling her he was going to take her home.

The ceremony had been brief but dignified, he told her. A relative of

Desmond Elliot had been present and had already gone back to London.

As if in a dream, she dressed and packed and waited obediently for Rory to collect her. He treated her like a delicate child.

On the aircraft he fastened her seat belt and then gave her Myles' wallet and said he also had his briefcase to give her after they had landed.

At Heathrow Jonathan appeared suddenly, and she felt stifled with helpers. Jonathan dealt with her own case and Myles' briefcase. She thanked young Rory as sincerely as she knew how and let Jonathan take over.

'My car,' she said. 'What about my car?'

'I'll send someone to fetch it if you give me the keys. Now, you are coming with me in my car. I'm taking you to Foresters if that is what you would like, or would you rather come and stay with me and Gayle?'

'Foresters, please Jonna,' Jenny pleaded. 'Mrs Sproson will look after me. You will take care of your Father's will and all his investments and suchlike, won't you?'

Jonathan drove very carefully and patted his mother's knee from time to time on the drive home.

When they arrived at the house, Mrs Sproson was waiting. The older woman instinctively took Jenny into her arms and tried to comfort her, then led her to the couch in the drawing room and suggested tea. They both shed tears and held each other silently.

A little later, after a few signatures on some documents in his possession, Jonathan explained, 'You don't have to do a thing. 'You are now a very rich woman, and Father had already signed over the bulk of his fortune to me months ago. We are both very lucky. You have a numbered account in Switzerland with a considerable amount of money in it. Don't you remember his asking you for signatures some time ago?'

'Yes I do vaguely,' she answered. 'Anyway, I know you will cope.'

The room was full of wonderful fresh flowers and Ming came mincing in to greet her miaowing loudly. She picked him up and hugged him and he purred and kneaded her thigh. It was so wonderful, such a relief to be home. She told Jonna to help himself to a drink and then go off back to his family.

'If you are sure,' he said. 'Ring if you need anything.'

'Your number is always engaged,' she said.

'Only because I was trying to get you,' he laughed.

They kissed and he took her car keys and said he would have her car delivered back to her very soon. She watched his car sweep out of the drive then she sank back and wept.

PART THREE

ELEVEN

After a week or so roaming about the house, lingering in the Orangerie, removing a leaf here, a dead flower there, Jenny felt more strongly than ever before the longing to go out to see Myles' only remaining relative, his half-sister Sheena in Cyprus.

She pulled herself up from a kneeling position and raced up to Myles' study. His leather bound address book was at hand on the desk top. What was the Greek's name? It began with a C, she was sure of that. She turned anxiously to the Cs – Carlton – Chapman – Chivers – at last, Christophedes.

That was it. Nikita and Sheena Christophedes, Box 13 Kyrenia, Cyprus. No telephone number.

She sat down right away and, taking a sheet of Myles' best thick white writing paper, wrote:-

Dear Sheena,

I am Jenny Lander, wife of Myles Lander. You may or may not have heard of Myles' accident and tragic death. It happened about two weeks ago in the south of France. His car hit a stone wall and he was killed instantly.

I have always wanted to come out to see you since you seemed to be his only remaining relative, but could never persuade him to make the journey, or even get in touch with you. I am so keen to meet you and your husband. Will you write and tell me if and when it would be convenient?

I hope you are both well and so look forward to meeting you.

Yours sincerely,

Jenny Lander.

About ten days later came a reply on bright mauve paper in a round childish hand. She had replied!

Dear Jenny,
　I was so very happy to receive your letter. I did not know Myles at all well, just knew of his existence, but am so sorry to hear of his death. Both Nikita and I would love you to come out and visit us. Come as soon as possible. Just let me know the date and time of arrival and the flight number. You can fly by Cyprus Airways to Nicosia where we will meet you. I am newly pregnant about which we are both delighted. I am very well and, so far, don't have morning sickness, and it would be lovely to have your company.
　With our love and best wishes.
　Sheena.

Jenny was overjoyed at this response and busied herself during the next few days arranging a flight, letting them know the date proposed date of her arrival with the flight number and time. She had made the booking to fly in about a week's time.

Next, she busied herself choosing the right clothes, buying presents for her new relatives and asking Jonna to drive her to the airport.

Jonathan was pleased and delighted at Jenny's decision and amazed at her recovery from his Father's death.

Mrs Sproson invited one of her old friends from her girlhood town to come down and stay with her so, with someone to keep her company and the dog and cat, Jenny knew she would be content.

Her old retainer had hired a London firm to come down and remove all Myles' clothes and belongings (except for those Jonna had picked out for himself), and had been able to hand Jenny a sizeable cheque which they sent off to the World Wild Life Fund.

Jonathan assured her that she would have no trouble getting money through a branch of Barclays in Kyrenia. Any money or travellers cheques she took with her she could always cash there.

She left on 3 April. The comfortable flight only took four hours and she was duly met by her new-found relations at Nicosia airport.

Almost immediately Jenny understood what Myles meant about the Greek. He was loudly dressed in a checked suit, gaudy tie and polished brown brogues as bright as conkers, and his fat face had an oily sheen to it.

Sheena was a short plump redhead with freckled face and too much jewellery. They were both very friendly, even demonstrative, and greeted her like a precious long lost family relative.

The journey, after collecting her luggage, took only twenty minutes on a winding road. Towards the end of the journey they climbed steeply then, on the crest of the hill, had a panoramic view of Kyrenia down below.

The harbour, the old castle and the cluster of houses – each washed in a pale colour – and everywhere masses of early flowering trees.

Their own house, obviously new, was a vast white place looking like a mosque and lying a few miles to the west of the town. It was opulently furnished. The ornate marble floors mostly covered with patterned rugs, but the furniture and curtains could have come straight from Harrods, and probably had. The bedroom in which she was to stay was very feminine with its Laura Ashley prints used for duvet covering and curtains and cushions. The small bathroom off it was all pink like a pink cave.

It was early evening, and Sheena asked if Jenny would like tea or a drink. Seeing a tray set with glasses and a bottle of golden wine, Jenny opted for the wine, which Nikita was pleased about and hastened to give her a glass.

For a while they spoke about Myles and his sad death, then Sheena explained that his mother had married again after his Father's death and she was the sole child of that marriage. Her Mother too had died when Sheena was only six and her Father was struck down and died of cancer a few years later.

Jenny asked Nikita about his business, and the Greek explained that he had the largest areas of orange and lemon groves on the island; whole hill-sides of olive trees and factories for canning all of these products.

He was also into fisheries. He exported to many countries and his business grew and flourished continuously.

Sheena lived in luxury with a cook and several maids. She was to go into a nursing home in Nicosia for the actual birth of her child and, when

73

she came back, there would be a fully trained Lebanese nurse to look after her and the child.

After an excellent dinner – chilled fish soup followed by Moussaka, then a rich creamy pastry – Jenny realised just how sleepy she was and asked to be excused if she went off to bed early. The others assured her it was a wise thing to do and Sheena saw her to her room and fondly kissed her goodnight.

Jenny slept without dreaming and was woken early the next morning by one of the maids called Katrina carrying a tray of tea. The girl smiled, put the tray on the bedside table and curtsied before leaving the room.

When she had bathed and dressed, Jenny went to find Sheena in the dining room. On the table was a big pot of coffee, toast and honey and Jenny assured her hostess this was exactly to her taste and sat down beside her. Nikita had already gone off to the factories, Sheena explained, but would be home for lunch. It would be a good morning to see the town. Jenny said she would love to do that.

Sheena had a small Fiat but was a nervous driver, so she asked Jenny if she would care to drive.

'I'd love to,' Jenny replied. 'Just point out the turnings and parking places and I will do the rest!'

Around the picturesque harbour were many ships, schooners and caiques and a few modern yachts, some of which looked shabby riding at anchor. The waterfront was crescent-shaped and paved with limestone blocks, crumbling in places but fascinating. Bars, cafés, barbers' parlours and a grander building with fancy striped awning called The Harbour Club, encircled the water and, between the buildings and the quay, jacaranda and giant eucalyptus trees flourished. There was such a sense of peace and repose in the atmosphere that Jenny was enchanted.

From the waterfront, alleys ran back up through the town lined with other taverns and barbers' shops. There was a small museum and many churches – many more than could ever be required. There were ships chandlers, grocery stores, shops displaying seamen's boots, peaked caps, cheap harsh wool navy jumpers, shoes and jeans. There was also a hospital, a police station, a post office where one collected one's mail, a covered market, a school, huge warehouses and a town hall. Most buildings looked very old and crumbly, or frankly falling to bits, and had obviously been so for hundreds of years. Beyond, higher up the hill-sides, could be seen little houses painted pink or white or blue.

After a long look around, Jenny wanted to go into a taverna for an ouzo or some other local drink, but Sheena looked doubtful at this. However, to please her new found relative, she allowed herself to be guided inside to a smoky bar on a corner near the Harbour Club. When a waiter came to their table Jenny asked for ouzo but Sheena only wanted coffee.

Leaning against the doorpost was a fisherman. His face, thin, white and exhausted under a dark peaked cap, was curiously attractive. He made Jenny think of Clint Eastwood. The almost finished cigarette stuck in the corner of his mouth, and the narrowed light golden eyes with a curious ring around the iris fascinated her. He wore the mandatory seaman's harsh blue jersey and narrow patched jeans tucked into high black boots. There was a silver ring on the little finger of his right hand and he leaned with a sort of studied insolence against the doorpost. Jenny had no idea why he attracted her, but he certainly did!

She finished her strong aniseed-tasting drink and wanted to call for more, but Sheena looked uncomfortable and wanted to leave the place. So, leaving some coins on the table, she rose and took the girl's hand and led her back to the car.

'Nikita will soon be home,' the girl said.

The sailor grinned as they passed him and Jenny could see that some of his teeth were broken in places, but they were strong and white.

Nikita was waiting for them when they reached the house and, on being told that Jenny liked ouzo, hastened to find a bottle and set it out with a beautiful crystal jug of water beside her. He seemed both pleased yet amused at her taste, and suggested his wife should try it. She grimaced and said she preferred the sweet white wine.

'You should take Jenny up the hill to see old Tante Helena,' he remarked after lunch. 'The doctor said you should do some walking; it would be good for you.'

'Who is this Tante Helena?' Jenny asked.

Nikita explained that the old Cypriot woman had been his nurse when he was a small boy. She was known as Tante because she had spent many years rearing the children of a wealthy French family in Beirut. She was always called Tante Helena there and spoke fluent French. On the island she was renowned for her remedies for all ailments and was treated with great respect. Nikita paid her a small pension and she lived in a little pink house with a few chickens in the yard half way up the hill to a village called Karmi. They could take the car and leave it in the village of Aiyous Georgius and walk from there.

Sheena agreed they should go the next day if it was fine.

The Greek bent over and fondled his wife proudly and patted her fattening stomach. He said he hoped the baby would be a boy for he dearly wanted to be sure of one to inherit his empire and continue the business. A smug, contented man Jenny thought, but recoiled when he tried to touch her. She did not know why.

The next day dawned fine so they set off. It was barely a quarter of a mile up the hill from where they had left the car but lazy Sheena groaned as they neared the small house.

Jenny could see that the old woman had other visitors as they drew closer. It was the tall fisherman and his family. Tante Helena held a red-faced and squealing baby in the crook of her arm and was reaching up to a shelf for a stone bottle. Taking a spoon she poured some dark coloured liquid into it, opened the baby's mouth and poured it down its throat. The squealing stopped and the old woman handed the child back to its Mother, a plump dark haired woman with eyes like black olives.

Milling around were several youngsters. The fisherman pointed and said, 'All my children. Two sons I have.'

Sheena introduced Jenny and she and Tante Helena started at once speaking in French. The old woman seemed pleased to be using the language again and made them welcome. The fisherman thanked her, collected a child on his shoulder and one under each arm while another hung on to his trouser leg, and they followed the Mother and baby out of the yard.

Tante Helena said how good it was for Sheena to have such a nice friend to spend time with whilst waiting for her confinement, and did not the friend think the lucky girl was fortunate to have such a fine rich husband?

Jenny agreed with her on all these points, then went on to ask about her own time spent in the Lebanon. Coffee was brewed for them, and sipped slowly during the conversation. However, Sheena seemed to be anxious to take her leave so Jenny reluctantly said goodbye and took her arm to help her on the descent.

As soon as they were out of earshot, Jenny asked what was the liquid the old woman had used to cure the baby's bad throat.

Sheena explained it was some sort of berry crushed and steeped in vinegar. 'You must know, in England, they use raspberry vinegar to cure any throat ailment.'

Jenny had heard her Mother speak of it, but it seemed somewhat drastic for such a young child.

Coming out of the compound, Jenny noticed the ruins of what might have been an old church higher on the hill above the village and thought one day she might go exploring by herself.

Back at the house, Sheena went to lie down and Jenny went to her room. She thought again about the fisherman and wondered what attracted her so. She thought of the strange eyes and the battered silver ring and how his hands were finely shaped.

She thought also about the old ruins and determined to ask Nikita about the place.

She found her chance when they met before dinner and he was pouring her some of the light golden wine. 'People say it is a bad place – has evil spirits which can do you harm. In my Father's day it is true they dug up treasures there. Some gold, silver, a few stones but no good came to the people who took them. More than that I do not know.'

'Is there no sort of clinic where the poor can take their children?' Jenny asked Sheena when she joined them.

'There is in the town near the hospital,' she said, 'but the people won't use it. They prefer the old remedies.'

'How does a poor fisherman feed his family?' she asked Nikita.

'They live very simply,' he said. 'A crust of bread with a little olive oil, goats' milk, melons, fruit, some cheap cheeses. They get by until the boats go out again for the next catch. It will be fat sardines the next time.'

One day Jenny thought that she would climb the mountain and see those ruins for herself – and maybe see the fisherman who lived, she believed, quite near Tante Helena.

She simply could not get the image of those sad oblique eyes out of her mind.

Dinner again was excellent. A strong clear consommé, then baby lamb chops grilled almost black around the edges over charcoal and a big rough coarse-leaved salad tossed in an unusual dressing. Jenny refused the rich cream pastry sweet and waited for the coffee, thick dark and rich as she had first encountered it in Istanbul.

After dinner they played backgammon. Nikita beat her every time but then, as he reminded her, he had been playing it since he was three. Only then it was called Trik-Trak.

One day Nikita drove her around his olive groves far to the west to a town called Morphou – and on another day to the canning factory.

One evening the three of them dined at the Harbour Club in great style. There was a smart bar and a small band with a singer. The food was not as good as that served at her relatives' home.

One morning when Sheena was feeling lazy and stayed in bed, Jenny drove herself down to the harbour, parked and went to the tavern where she had first tasted ouzo.

She sipped her drink slowly, hoping to see the sad fisherman, but there was no sign of him. She was greatly disappointed.

One night when she could not get off to sleep, she got up and went into her bathroom for a glass of water. Returning with it to her bed she heard a gentle tapping at her door. She opened it to find Nikita in loudly striped pyjamas squeezing into her room.

He put out his hand onto her shoulder and said, 'I wondered if there was anything you wanted.'

The inference was offensive, and she felt herself recoiling from his touch. She shuddered and pushed him firmly out of the room. She lay panting with indignation for a long time until at last she slept.

The following day she resumed her normal attitude towards him but she knew he had taken her repulse badly.

She asked him something about the political problems on the island but his explanations were far too complicated for her to understand clearly. She understood for herself Makarios was a better politician than a priest, and that he wanted union with Greece. She only knew that she didn't like the idea of holy men having helicopters. There was talk of another party wanting union with Turkey, but for the most part it was beyond her comprehension. Apart from this, Nikita was not keen to discuss the matter.

One day she drove herself into Nicosia, took a walk down Ledra Street and was fascinated by the endless small shops selling pretty junk jewellery – both Greek and Turkish – bracelets, bangles, rings and necklaces. She bought a number of colourful pieces with Lulu, Gayle and Filly in mind. Afterwards she had a charmingly served snack lunch at a very grand hotel called The Ledra Palace and afterwards found a library where she took out membership and came away with two books, Lawrence Durrell's *Bitter Lemons* and another about the ruins of the old Abbey at Bellapais.

That evening at dinner she mentioned she would like to see the old Abbey. and Nikita promised to take them both to this and afterwards to lunch at Ambelia which was a cleverly constructed replica of an old Cypriot village run as an hotel.

This happened three days later when Nikita had some time to spare. The ancient ruins of the Abbey, with its impressive arches and wonderful views was fascinating and they had a drink at the café near The Tree of Idleness where crowds of old men sat day by day gossiping and smoking.

Ambelia proved equally attractive in a very different way. An architect had reproduced a typical Cypriot village with a paved street of yellow stone with houses each a different shape on either side and, below, near a superb turquoise swimming pool, a row of studio flats. There was also a bar and restaurant where they had lunch and looked down over the town and harbour.

Some gentle music, probably from a stereo, was playing in the background and climbing flowers proliferated.

Above all, Jenny marvelled at the peace and utter calm of the place; everything here moved at a snail's pace. A tranquillity rarely found in the world today was certainly here. The waiters glided about their duties, the well-fed cats stretched out on the warm stones and all was peace.

She felt she could lie there all afternoon reflecting on things in general – there was no need to hurry. Nobody did.

TWELVE

It was clearly Spring now. The air each day seemed to grow warmer. Everything grew greener, more little goats were born, each one exquisite and adorable in their cartoon-like perfection, but weak, so touchingly weak and trembly.

Jenny began to wonder about the possibility of swimming, and asked Nikita about the beaches. He told her there were many lovely golden sandy ones all along the Pan Handle to the East. He suggested she take Sheena's car and see for herself. Sheena, who did not swim and burned very easily in the breeze and midday sun, urged her to go off and explore.

The next morning, in glorious sunshine, she set off at ten o'clock and followed the winding narrow road beyond Kyrenia. She stopped at the first inlet, but remembering Nikita had said the Twelve Mile Beach was the best, drove on until she came to a sign indicating it.

Down a rutted, pot-holed road the small car bumped and jolted until suddenly rounding a bend Jenny saw a wonderful expanse of golden sand. The tide was in and to her left was a series of jutting blue-grey rocks, some smoothed and flattened by the splash of the tide so that one could lie comfortably and look down on quite deep water. The sea was very blue with white horses at intervals stretching out to the horizon.

She had put on a swimsuit when she dressed, so now just simply whipped off her blouse and skirt and, leaving them far back on the sand, climbed and stretched out on the warm smooth rock.

This, she sighed, was the sort of beach she had always longed for during holidays abroad with Myles. Wild, deserted and unspoiled.

She lay sunning herself and thinking about the fisherman. It was not easy to define her thoughts about him. She felt somehow instinctively that he too was frustrated, embittered by life. He attracted her in a way no

80

other man had ever done. There was something in his eyes, in his expression that matched her own feelings. A hopeless longing, a regret. She so needed to see him again.

After a while she climbed down from the rocky shelf and lay on the rippled sand at the edge of the water. It was so very soothing, letting each wave wash over her body. It was soothing, calming, caressing.

After a while she got to her feet and climbed back on the rocks and jumped off into the deep water. She swam vigorously around them, backwards and forwards, and at last back to the beach again where she lay breathing deeply and feeling pleasantly tired and let the shallow waves wash over her.

Then she rubbed herself down with her towel and put on her clothes. If she hurried, she had time to stop off at the taverna again before going back to the house for lunch.

She would come down here again tomorrow. It was so perfect. Walking barefoot along the edge of the waves she bent and picked up many blue and green stones, but once out of the water they were all disappointingly grey. She tossed them back.

Driving quickly back to Kyrenia, she parked the car in the same spot Sheena had previously indicated and made her way into the dark taverna near the Harbour Club.

The gaunt man was there. She motioned to him to come to her table and asked him what he would like to drink.

'Strega,' he said quietly and she was tempted to try it but asked for ouzo. A waiter brought the drinks.

'What is your name?' she asked the silent man.

'Spiros,' he said shyly.

'I am Jenny,' she told him.

'You are one crazy woman Jinny.'

'Why?'

'Coming in here – drinking with one no-good seaman,' he said.

'Where did you learn your English?' she asked.

'Many years ago – I am in Greece – merchant boat. I learn plenty, many bad bad words. I want I speak better. I sorry.'

'No, it's wonderful you speak any English at all,' Jenny said. 'When will you be going to sea again?'

81

'When is time for sardines – soon now,' he replied.

'I want very much to see the old ruins above Karmi – would you be my guide? You live somewhere near Tante Helena, don't you?'

'Yes, very near,' he answered.

'How is the baby now.'

'He strong. Very well, like me,' he said, thumping his chest.

'I shall try to go up there tomorrow afternoon if the weather is fine,' she said quietly, finishing her ouzo. 'Maybe you will climb up with me.'

'Sure-sure I be waiting for you past Tante Helena place,' he said.

'Until tomorrow then,' Jenny said.

'You no want more ouzo?' he begged.

'No – I must go. I must hurry. My family will be waiting for me.'

She put a note down on the table under her glass and stood up. He touched the peak of his cap and looked at her with pleading eyes.

Jenny hurried back to the car.

'You look quite pink from the sun. I hope you are not burned,' Nikita said. They had waited lunch for her and she apologised.

She was loud in her praises of Twelve Mile Beach, describing how she had jumped off the rocks and swum vigorously.

Nikita told her that was dangerous. 'Many undercurrents. You should go into the sea from the beach,' he said.

'I am always careful and a very strong swimmer,' she told them. Then she changed the subject and admired Sheena's embroidery. She was covering a pillow slip with blue and pink flowers from a transfer. The pattern included some baby animals.

'The weekend after next is a Festival,' Nikita said. 'We always give a party with big iced cakes and many fairy lights and dancing,' he added. 'You will see some of the local dances and the Zorba danced by the men. I hope you will enjoy that.'

'But I haven't brought any party clothes. What on earth shall I wear?' she asked Sheena.

'Oh, I can lend you a pretty pale blue linen Greek dress embroidered in black. I can't get into it now and it will suit you very well.'

'How kind you are to me,' Jenny exclaimed, bending over and kissing her fondly.

'I shall just wear my stretchy skirt and a frilly white blouse,' Sheena said. 'You can help me with the decorations.'

'Gladly,' Jenny replied. 'Now I must go and take off my swim suit and take a shower.'

Going down the passage to her room, Nikita caught her arm and said, 'What is all this drinking in the bars with young Spiros?'

'Quite harmless. I just like ouzo and find him interesting,' she answered.

'It is not a good idea. People talk. I have my spies. Please, while you are in my house, you must observe the formalities.'

'Really, Nikita, I am a middle-aged woman. I will not be dictated to,' she said, anger mounting in her voice.

He turned away saying no more.

The next morning she set off earlier for her swim but, on reaching the Twelve Mile Beach, was annoyed to see a man lying on her favourite rock. She took off her things and lay on the rippled sand letting the waves wash over her body. Then, wading out into deeper water, she swam energetically for ten minutes or so. As she left the sea, the man who had been lying on her rock got up and walked towards her. He was of medium height with a muscular tanned body and faded blond hair. She judged him to be about her own age.

'I hope I haven't stolen your favourite beach,' he said. 'I am staying at Ambelia. The pool there is excellent. I have been too lazy to find the sea.'

'I don't blame you. I have seen it and thought it most attractive,' she answered.

'I am Nick Henderson,' the man said, and held out his hand.

She took it in her wet one and said, 'My name is Jenny Lander. I am staying with relatives. How do you do? What are you doing in Cyprus so early in the year?'

'My wife died recently of cancer and I have been given a month's leave to recuperate. I lecture at Manchester University. This is the most healing and peaceful place I know, he said.

'Yes. The pace of life is so slow. It seems as if nothing has changed in hundreds of years.'

'I fear there is going to be trouble before very long,' he said.

'I am afraid I am totally ignorant of the politics of the island,' Jenny admitted. 'I, too, am seeking recuperation – staying with relatives just the other side of Kyrenia.'

'Perhaps we may meet again some other day,' he said with a shy smile.

'Yes, More than likely. I really must dash now or I shall be late for lunch. *Au revoir.*'

'*Au revoir*,' he replied.

Driving much too fast along the bad road, she parked near the quay and hurried into the dingy little taverna. There was no sign of Spiros. She quickly drank up her ouzo and left the bar.

At lunch she recounted her meeting with the Englishman. Nikita said, 'You must invite him to the house. We would be pleased to see him, especially Sheena. She would enjoy the company of a new man.'

'Thank you. If I do meet him at the beach again I certainly will pass on your invitation. You could of course always contact him at Ambelia.'

'That's a very good idea. I think I will do that. When would you like him to come, Sheena darling?'

'Try to get in touch with him and ask him for dinner tomorrow evening,' Sheena said.

After lunch, when Nikita had gone back to work, Sheena went to bed to rest and the whole house was quiet.

Jenny put on a loose light weight peasant skirt and thin cashmere sweater. With comfortable shoes she decided not to take the car but to walk all the way. It took her about twenty minutes to the village and then she began her climb.

The sun had gone in but around her as she climbed were all the signs of Spring. The grass was greener and here, and there were great patches, myriads of tiny brightly coloured wild flowers. A few fat-tailed sheep and many goats with their enchanting babies in black and white or black and tan and a few all black. Each one was perfect and so like the Disney pictures Jenny felt herself wanting to catch one and cuddle it, but of course they pranced and jumped out of reach. Next came a shepherd with saddlebags riding a poor old donkey.

Still walking, she saw no one until she rounded a grassy knoll and saw him. She was almost out of breath by now and almost fell into his arms.

He realised her fatigue and pulled her gently to lean against him.

In some confusion she looked deep into his eyes and breathlessly said, 'I am so stupid. I hurried up the hill you see because I thought you may get tired of waiting and go away . . .'

'For you Jinny – I wait for ever.'

Suddenly he looked embarrassed and took his hands from her shoulders and guided her to lean against a craggy boulder overhanging the dried bed of a small stream. In a flash she realised that he had no idea of her conception of him. She looked up at his face. He had the inevitable cigarette stub in the corner of his mouth. Immediately he pulled the stub out and ground it underfoot.

'OK now?' he said jauntily and tucked his thumbs into his belt.

'All right now. Let's go on,' she said, now breathing normally.

They began to walk side by side, or rather climb, for the track grew very steep. The earth was badly scarred in places, tufted thick growths of nettles and thistles impeded their way. They encountered the odd dusty-looking sheep. Here and there an odd olive tree, odd patches of tufted grass. She wanted to ask him so much. How did the farmers, the owners of the peculiar fat-tailed sheep make a living? But she did not know how to begin.

They continued up hill in single file now. She could see his thin shoulders moving and the attractive slant of his high cheek bone. His cap was tipped back, his thumbs still stuck in the narrow belt of his tight pants. They climbed for half an hour in silence.

'OK?' his voice came from somewhere above her. He was looking down at her with that amused shaky grin. She had to sit down to steady her breathing. Her heart was beating loud and fast. After a while she felt steadier, rose and willed herself to move more quickly.

When she next looked up she found that they had reached the ruins.

'See!' he said, triumphantly. 'See!' His voice had a bold ring to it. 'This I tell you was one fine church and there one big fine house!'

Among the blind grey stones he stood like a prince. She scrambled to reach him and he held out a hand.

The place had been abandoned for many centuries. An old well-head, square and black, stood nearby. They looked down and saw the sky mirrored many many feet below.

'Many things down there – gold – jewels – rings. They was all rich then, I tell you.'

He began scrabbling in the earth beside them. After a while he picked up a fragment of glass, iridescent, very fragile, very thin. He rubbed it gently on his sleeve and gave it to her.

'That's nothing,' he said, 'but plenty stuff down there, plenty, I tell you. You ask Christophedes, he know.'

'But what did they find?' she asked.

'You ask him, the fat one, he tell you.'

It had grown darker now. The clouds had lowered. She saw a silver lizard on a stone. It darted away. They went deeper into the chapel and faced a great blank wall. Spiros took a short stick and, dipping it in the reddish earth, wrote his name in beautiful Greek letters.

Then he came towards her. She clenched her fist and the forgotten piece of glass broke against her ring and cut a finger, so that when he took her in his arms there was blood on his face too. The rain, so long threatening, began to fall.

She was never sure afterwards whether she lost consciousness – she only knew that she cried, giving herself up to whatever may happen and what happened was the most wonderful thing she had ever experienced in her whole life. The actual physical release from such long celibacy was fierce, brutal. She knew now that never before had she experienced an orgasm, such deep joy.

He was amazed, frightened at what he had done. Her weeping terrified him. His act appeared to him blasphemous, partly because they were in a chapel. Yet he too had never known such joy. Jenny wept on and on because she could not help it. She knew now that she was hopelessly and absolutely in love with this man, that no good could ever come of it. She continued to weep in sheer disgust for her own helpless femininity.

Spiros, on his knees stroked her wet face, sucked the finger that was bleeding. With shaking hands he muttered barely understandable words. 'Did I hurt you – you want I go away now?' Then in Greek he was calling her softly – a flower – a jewel. His passion and his tenderness afterwards was unlike anything she could have expected.

She felt astonished, deeply touched by his sweetness and, through her tears, she smiled up at him, speaking his name in gratitude. She touched his face, his streaky fine hair, getting to know the sound and feel of him. He found a red spotted handkerchief and dabbed at her face, then took her bleeding finger into his mouth and sucked it clean. She let him kneel

86

beside her straightening her clothes, pulling off his rough jersey and wrapping it around her shoulders.

This is being in love, she told herself. The smell of wild thyme was powerful, and there was a faint odour of incense. She simply couldn't believe that she could feel such happiness when it was clear that the situation was impossible.

'You are one mad woman Jinny,' he said. 'Jinny – ah – Jinny.'

He looked suddenly very shy, very gauche. She took a deep breath and got to her feet.

'We must go,' she said. 'I will go down first alone. I will look for you tomorrow in the harbour taverna. Here – take this.' She pulled the heavy platinum ring from her index finger and pushed it on the little finger of his left hand – then she took the old battered silver ring from his finger and put it on her index finger. 'It is made of platinum,' she told him. 'More expensive than gold – ask any jeweller. Until tomorrow then. You keep it to remember me.' She pressed his hand and slipped away down the hill.

'Wait – wait!' he yelled, running after her. She paused. 'Not old taverna. Go round corner ask for Homer's bar. Go in back room. I fix it with Homer.'

She turned and pushed his jersey into his hands, smiled once more and was gone.

All was silent in the Greek household. She crept into her room, took off her clothes and showered. As she washed her hair she thought wildly, hopefully, that perhaps she had conceived. She would know soon if she were pregnant. She was forty-six, but then, many famous actresses had had babies in their forties. She was very healthy. She went down on her knees and prayed: 'Please, please, dear God, let me be pregnant.'

She put on fresh clothes, dried and brushed her shining hair. Catching a glint of grey, she thought, I am too old.

When she went in to dinner she had pink cheeks and sparkling eyes.

'So, walking in the hills is good for you,' Nikita said, and poured her a glass of golden wine.

THIRTEEN

Glancing out of a window on her way to the dining room, she noticed a strange car parked at the side of the house. It was one she had not seen before – a bright pillar-box red. There must be visitors. The dining room was empty, but an extra place was set at the table. In the sitting room there was chatter and laughter.

Nick Henderson stood up. He was wearing a black sweater and white, slim trousers, casual but elegant. Nikita had been quick off the mark and obviously contacted him at Ambelia. He held out his hand to her, admiration in his glance.

Jenny, in her favourite blue dress with her sapphires, was looking her very best. She felt incandescent with love, her newly washed hair brushed into a shining halo round her face, her eyes more brilliant than the jewels. Even Nikita remarked that he thought hill climbing suited her!

Nick Henderson seemed struck dumb, and could not take his eyes off her. Of course, she told herself, the first time he had seen her was coming out of the water like a half-drowned cat. Nikita and Sheena both watched the two of them with interest. Nikita was smugly pleased with himself, having found a suitable man for her, and Sheena was intrigued too, to watch Jenny's reaction. If only they knew, Jenny thought to herself, and began to recount her discovery of the ruins.

After they went in to dinner she animated herself charmingly to entertain their new visitor, and knew that Nick Henderson was deeply attracted to her. She felt elated and eagerly drank the wine with which Nikita kept filling her glass.

Nick Henderson simply couldn't take his eyes off her. Their guest stayed until midnight and, on leaving, kissed Jenny's hand and said they must all come up to dine with him at Ambelia very soon. Nikita said he would get in touch.

Jenny swayed a little as she walked to her room, but she knew it wasn't only the wine which had caused her ecstasy, it was her afternoon's experience.

She undressed quickly and lay on her bed and relived her lover's every movement. To stop loving him now was beyond her. At last she slept and dreamed of Spiros.

Waking early she worked out in her mind how she could possibly help her lover. She could not insult him by giving him money, but since she had stolen him from his family, she could help his wife and children.

At breakfast she asked Sheena if she could borrow her car yet again and, waiting until ten o'clock when the bank in Kyrenia would be open, drove quickly there and asked to see the manager. In his office she asked him if she might put through a call to the bank in Beaconsfield. He agreed at once and calculated the time difference for her. She must wait an hour and in the meantime he would find the telephone number for her.

Meanwhile, she went across the road to the vast hotel called The Dome and sipped coffee and watched the few early visitors.

Back in the bank she found her personal call had come through and she spoke to her local bank manager. She asked him to arrange to make it possible for her to transfer two thousand pounds to her bank in Kyrenia. The man asked her to pass the phone to the local manager and they exchanged a few brief sentences.

'Your money is available to you now,' the manager said.

'Then I have a strange request,' Jenny said. 'I want two thousand Cypriot pounds in notes of small denomination packed into a big plastic bag to take away with me.'

'No trouble, madam,' the neat Cypriot man assured her. 'I will quickly arrange that.'

Jenny sat down in the manager's office and presently a clerk came to her with a bulky plastic package. She thanked him and the manager and, taking the bundle, went quickly back to the car.

Driving back towards the village of Ayios Georgios she decided to go and see Tante Helena who would certainly help her.

Fortunately, the old woman was alone. They chatted in French for a few minutes and then Jenny explained that she wanted to help the fisherman's family as discreetly as possible. She put the bag of bank notes into Helena's lap and begged her to give the money, a wad at a time, to Christella to buy food, shoes and clothes for the children. She must also buy herself some pretty dresses and materials for making the special white cakes with the silver balls for the next Saints' Day party.

'I want to help this family,' she explained. 'I cannot insult his pride by giving it to the man, but you can explain that a well-wisher wants to help his family. Will you do that for me?'

'Gladly, my dear,' Tante Helena said, and smiled an understanding smile.

'I'm so grateful to you,' Jenny said humbly.

'I shall send the next small boy I see with a message to Christella to come and see me.'

'I shall be going back to England soon,' Jenny explained, 'and you are the only true friend I have. Bless you and thank you so very much. Goodbye now. I will try to see you once more before I leave.'

Driving back to the harbour, Jenny parked the car and sat for a long time on the sea wall watching the slow moving activities around her. At midday she made her way to the taverna round the corner and, as Spiros had told her, soon found Homer's bar.

Homer was a short fat old man with a deeply lined face and kind hazel eyes. He lifted a section of the bar and drew her through to a small back room, following her with a bottle of wine and some glasses. He went back and brought a dish of green olives and some fetta cheese.

After closing the door, Jenny looked around and saw that the room contained a wide couch, a table and two chairs. Some rather limp curtains barely covered the windows which in fact only looked out on the back of a small church. Another door gave onto a narrow passage which led to a Turkish style toilet and nearby a small wash basin with a single cold water tap.

A few minutes later there was a light tap on the bar door and Spiros came in. He took her in his arms and she felt her heart beat quicken and happiness flood over her.

FOURTEEN

When she went back for lunch, she told Sheena and Nikita that she thought it time she thought about returning to England.

They both seemed surprised, and Nikita said, 'I thought that now you have found a suitable male companion you would be contented to stay at least until Nick Henderson goes.'

'Oh, so you have been in touch with him again?'

'Yes, and I have accepted his invitation for all of us to dine with him at Ambelia tomorrow evening. Does that not please you?'

'Thank you, yes. I shall book a flight early next week.'

Husband and wife looked at each other questioningly. 'I was so hoping you would stay with me until the birth,' Sheena said plaintively.

'Unfortunately, there are several things at home I must attend to,' Jenny said quietly, but made no effort to define them.

She made no more journeys to the beach, but started instead to give all her time to helping her sister-in-law with preparations for the party.

'Don't you want to see Nick any more?' Sheena asked.

'No, quite frankly he bores me.'

'Oh, I find him very attractive,' Sheena confessed, 'but I never dare say so in front of Nikita. He made it very obvious that he is smitten with you at Ambelia the other evening,' Sheena said.

'Sorry, I found his efforts to please me absolutely sickening,' Jenny replied.

For the party a great area of the garden was cleared and levelled for dancing. Jenny watched as men climbed and hung gaudy lanterns in the tallest trees. Strings of fairy lights criss-crossed the dancing arena and beside it, long trestle tables were covered with starched linen cloths. Piles and piles of plates and crates of glasses were put on them and on another

91

the knives, forks and spoons, napkins and bottles of wine. The cooking of the sheep was to be done further back where beds of charcoal were built and spits arranged.

Jenny helped Sheena make big colourful flowers from sheets and sheets of crepe paper and these were pinned in every spot available. A huge radiogram with a turntable stood in the hall with speakers distributed around the grounds and Sheena found stacks of old records – Greek, English and American – which she placed near the machine.

The weather the following day was fine. The maids were busy making the big iced festive cakes with silver balls and many bowls of trifle, or its equivalent, filled the big fridge.

As soon as dusk fell, the revelry and the roasting and dancing began. Everyone in the town that day was dressed up in some sort of costume, some with masks.

It was incongruous to hear plaintive Greek tunes and next, Elvis Presley and someone demanding, 'To dance again like we did last Summer.' Streamers of all colours were thrown criss-cross over the arena and people sang and shouted. The wine flowed.

Nikita was dressed like a Greek soldier in tutu skirt, legs like hams, feet thrust into slippers with red pom-poms on the toes. Sheena had made Jenny don a diaphanous head-dress, a sort of tiara with the filmy fabric draped across it and falling to her shoulders. On this Sheena sprinkled glittering silver powder. She herself had donned an embroidered waistcoat over her pretty blouse and her plump tummy was all the more obvious. She had also donned a black velvet mask.

Very quickly the roasting and turning of the sheep on the spits was well on its way and a sort of conga of people had formed and were dancing across the ground and into the house and out through another door.

From time to time, the dancers paused to drink a glass of wine and then get back into line and danced on. Jenny joined in and found herself enjoying the craziness of it all. The evening was warm and the heat from the glowing charcoal made the atmosphere hotter still. Jenny drank a full glass of retsina, then joined the line and entered the house. For a moment she broke the line to open a window.

Below she saw a face. It was unmistakeably the face of Spiros. He was disguised as an animal and had pulled aside his mask. He beckoned her to come and join him but Jenny looked wildly around and saw Nikita with a bottle of whisky. He drank some and then swayed on his feet.

She crept outside to find Spiros and, when she did, made him fasten his mask again. They hurled themselves into the chain of dancers again feeling more than a little intoxicated. Jenny loved the feel of Spiros' hands clutching her hips and gave herself up to the crazy atmosphere, but when she saw Nikita again she knew she had to insist on Spiros leaving the party or murder might be done.

He listened to her whispered appeal and, after one snatched embrace in the shelter of a plumbago bush, hurried away obediently.

Nikita came over and seized Jenny in a fierce embrace and whirled her into the frenzied dance pressing his great fat stomach against her until she cried out.

'We cannot leave Sheena all alone, we must go to her,' Jenny gasped, and tore herself away.

Fortunately it was time to eat. Great slices of succulent mutton were passed around on plates. The very smell of it made Jenny feel sick, but she found a plate of cheese and some green olives and made a meal of these. Nikita brought her another glass of wine and soon it was time for the Zorba dance.

Eight men in various stages of intoxication moved as one to the haunting tune. The back-stepping, the crossing of the legs, the hesitation and the passings and knee dipping was a splendid sight. Jenny loved the Zorba music and tried hard to memorise the intricate steps. She vowed she would get Sheena to show her.

More paper streamers shot across over the heads of the gathering and then it was time to cut the celebration cakes. Once more Chubby Checker begged them all to 'dance again like we did last Summer' and the white and silver cakes were consumed with relish.

In a pause, Jenny asked Nikita again about the treasures found in the ruins up the hill.

'Oh, it was a very long time ago; many, many years before the war. Many, many plates one of my uncles had. He sent them to London for examination then gave them to a museum. I don't remember hearing of any jewels. A few fragments perhaps. A collar studded with rubies and a tiara, but no good ever came to the people who wore them. Hence the

93

fable of evil spirits.'

'I would like a tiara and a snake bracelet too,' Sheena said.

'Then I shall buy them for you, my love,' Nikita declared. 'One day when we go to London with our son – we shall *all* go to London.' His voice was thick and slurred.

The dance had started up again and Jenny rejoined the crowd. She joined a circle who were leaping and dipping, gliding forward and back. One girl stood alone in the centre of a circle and each one in the ring danced forward and kissed the hem of her skirt. Then they all stopped for a drink. Nikita had brought over more bottles and glasses on a tray to the sweating throng.

Jenny darted away to help Sheena to her room – she was looking distinctly weary. She helped her to undress and then lay down on the great wide bed beside her. After a while they both slept from sheer exhaustion.

In the morning they woke and laughed together. When Jenny returned to her own room she found Nikita in her bed and laughed helplessly. Such a lucky escape.

Gathering up a few clothes she went back to Sheena's bathroom, washed and dressed, then helped her sister-in-law to do the same. She did not mention Nikita.

In the dining room was a tray with fresh hot coffee and newly baked rolls and honey. The two chatted and laughed about the party. Neither of them mentioned Nikita.

Jenny decided she would like one last swim and, asking Sheena's blessing, took the little car and headed for her favourite beach. It was a perfect day and she had the rocks to herself. She lay and thought of Spiros and prayed again that she might be pregnant.

FIFTEEN

Jenny booked her flight from the travel agent in the Dome hotel. It was to be in three day's time. On the day before her departure she went to the little room in Homer's bar for the last time.

When she told Spiros she was leaving, he went down on his knees and begged her to stay, but she told him that the situation had become impossible. Vaguely at the back of her mind she had plans to do something really important to help her lover – perhaps even buy him a boat, but it was the vaguest, wildest idea. She knew only that she could ask Jonathan to help her look into the possibilities.

As they clung together for the last time, she begged him to leave the tavern first and give her enough time to get back to her car alone.

Blinded by tears, she mumbled her thanks to old Homer and pressed a bundle of notes into his hand, then stumbled from the place to find the car.

There were more tears from Sheena when the actual day of the flight came, but the girl promised to write and, sobbing, thanked her for her friendship and company.

She had already phoned Jonathan giving him date, flight number and time of arrival so that he would be sure to meet her at Heathrow.

Nikita even shed a few tears as they saw her off at Nicosia airport and said he hoped she would come back to see their baby son when he had been born.

Little did any of them know then of the ugly disastrous events which were to overtake them.

The flight was uneventful. Jenny could neither sleep nor eat. She sipped incipid coffee and tried to control her tears.

At Heathrow, she flung herself into Jonna's arms and wept unashamedly.

95

He was completely mystified as she only muttered that she was afraid disaster may overtake the island and was worried about the safety of her new-found relatives. Jonathan tried to reassure her, but without the slightest success. He did admit there were rumours of trouble.

Once home at Foresters, welcomed as always by Mrs Sproson, Jenny let her tears flow and was hugged and comforted by the old woman.

Jonathan had to leave for a bank meeting but promised to come over again at the weekend and discuss the subject of Cyprus with his Mother.

After a comforting, warm, scented bath Mrs Sproson tucked Jenny up in her bed and closed the curtains. Taking her suitcase, she unpacked quietly in an adjoining room and tip-toed away.

Jenny slept for a few hours then rushed to the bathroom to see if she had started her period. She was to do this ten times a morning for several days, dreading the sight of blood.

When on the fifth day after her return she found she had begun bleeding she was heart broken. She had wanted a child so passionately she was inconsolable. She lost weight and Mrs Sproson, concerned for her condition, fed her cream-filled chicken soup and many appetising and nourishing meals, but she became thinner.

Wild schemes started forming in her mind. Why should she not, with Spiros' permission, adopt one of his sons. The second one was most like him and presently aged about six. He had his Father's strange pale gold eyes with the black-rimmed irises. His name, she remembered, was Mandis. He had his Mother's thick black curly hair, but his features were his Father's. She would bring him up with the utmost care, see that he had the finest education and become qualified to help his Father's family.

Next she thought that, since she was a rich woman, perhaps she should buy Spiros a boat of his own, but she had no idea of the cost or how to begin to investigate the project. Jonathan would help her.

She would tell Jonathan that she had decided to look after a poor fisherman's family as her life's charity and he would begin to understand her motives and begin to see the wisdom of her actions. After all, his own Father had taken good care that he himself should never be short of money. His Mother should be allowed to be free to make her own choice as to what she should do with her money.

When on his next visit she broached the subject, he warned her it may prove to be complicated, but he would begin to make enquiries. The possibilities of such a project would have to be very carefully researched, but he would do his best to help her.

Christmas came and the usual rituals were observed. The lit-up tree, the present giving, the carving of the turkey and the well-scrubbed twenty-pence pieces hidden in the children's portions of Christmas pudding. Games were played, quarrels brewed, tears were shed. The drawing room looked like a jumble sale. Ben and Ming tore all the paper hats to shreds and at last it was over.

After Jenny and Mrs Sproson had restored the house to order, Jenny felt inclined to start her editing again but delayed for she felt more important work for her was soon to begin.

One day, as she and Mrs Sproson were having their lunch in the kitchen, her old friend said, 'I think you should call me Ethel.'

Jenny replied, 'No, you will always be Mrs Sproson to me and that is what I shall always call you. On the other hand I think you should call me Jenny, for you have been like a Mother to me for such a long, long time.'

'All right, if that is what you want. I have always thought of you as Jenny since the first time you were brought to the house.'

Jenny leaned over and kissed the rosy-cheeked woman and was touched to see tears in her eyes.

'Oh dear, I have agreed to go and spend a few days over at Barnes with the family, and I'm not looking forward to it,' Jenny moaned. Picking up her beloved little cat she buried her face in his pale coat and cuddled him.

'Better go soon and get it over with,' Mrs Sproson advised.

Jenny followed her advice and rang up to see if it was convenient to visit, and left for the visit the next day.

Timothy was delighted to see her and she him, for Jenny had to admit to herself she did not care for the female members of the family.

She stayed three days until it was time for Timmy to go back to school and then left on the pretext that there was a lot of work to be done in the Orangerie.

So, for weeks she pruned and repotted and bought and installed various new tropical flowering plants and found the work soothing.

Jonathan rang her from time to time explaining how very complex it was to buy a fishing boat near Spiros' village. He really needed to go out to the island himself to organise the purchase and, as Jenny realised this would mean letting Nikita in on her secret gesture, told him to forget the idea, she would think of something else.

Jonathan readily agreed to advise her how to instruct the Swiss Bank to send two hundred pounds per month to Nikita and meanwhile she herself would write and explain to Nikita this money was for him to give to Christella for use for the children.

Nikita replied by return of post, and promised to gladly carry out this task for her.

Jenny read in the newspapers that the political atmosphere on the island was tense, and she realised the time for Sheena's confinement was growing near.

She spent some time with Lulu and her family and went up to London to see a special exhibition at Burlington House, but was not tempted enough to buy anything.

June dragged on until, in July, on the twenty-first, she heard over the radio that the island had been invaded by a strong Turkish army force, also with parachutists and bombers. Various strenuous enquiries about the well-being of her relatives produced nothing.

But at the end of the month a badly written letter in Sheena's round, childish hand assured her that they were all safe in Paphos in the south of the island. Nikita had collected Tante Helena and Spiros' family in one of his lorries and driven them down to the south. Spiros had been killed hand-to-hand fighting in the harbour area. Sheena's labour pains had started as soon as they reached the south and Nikita, who was well known to members of the Royal Air Force station at Akrotiri, had driven her quickly over to the hospital there. After only four hours in labour, she had given birth to a fine, healthy baby boy. Now they were all temporarily housed in a hotel in Paphos, and Nikita intended building a house on some land he already owned there. He also owned some orange groves which had been neglected, but could be restored.

Jenny answered with lavish gifts, and sent flowers through InterFlora, but had no idea if any of these ever reached their destination.

She sat at the kitchen table with her old friend and watched the old woman's face as Mrs Sproson said, 'There is only one thing I regret in my life – I just wish I'd 'ad a couple of kids.'

'Don't we all,' said Jenny.

SIXTEEN

Now that Spiros was dead, she found herself dwelling more and more on the possibility of adopting one of his sons. Only this would solve her inner turmoil and make life worth living. She spoke briefly to Jonathan about the idea and he said he thought the adoption of a war orphan would be viewed favourably by the Home Office or the immigration authorities, and she should have no trouble.

She spent several sleepless nights mulling over the project, and came to the conclusion that she must do the thing honestly and go out and see Christella and, with Tante Helena's help, put the proposition to the young woman herself. She might not agree to giving up one of her children. It must be her decision that counted.

Cyprus Airways told her when she rang them that flights to a new airfield were being started shortly. They would let her know when she could book a seat. The new airport was to be at Larnaca. She could stay at an hotel in Limassol a few miles south. Paphos was already overcrowded. She could hire a small car and see her relatives and Spiros' family daily.

Another letter from Sheena told her Nikita had found housing for the Josephides – she had never known Spiros' surname until now – and Tante Helena on the ground floor of what used to be a big warehouse. He had put in beds and rugs and a hot water cistern. They were well-placed near the market and the small infants' school. With a feeling of guilt and regret, Jenny came to realise what a great-hearted, caring man Nikita was. She had sadly maligned and doubted him. From now on she would trust him and value his excellent work.

A week went by and, at last, the airline said she could book a flight any Wednesday or Saturday from now on. She rang back and booked a seat in one week's time.

During that week she went on a gigantic shopping spree, buying dresses for Christella, whom she judged to be a size sixteen, and many toys for the children. A football, a Leggo set and dolls for the little girls.

For Tante Helena she bought an elegant light-weight but warm black wrap with fringed ends. Next, a huge box of chocolates.

Jenny decided to persuade Sheena, the baby and the nursemaid to come over to England and occupy the ideal nursery suite. If her wish over the boy was granted, he could travel with the family and Mrs Sproson would have everything in order and ready for them. Her capable housekeeper had already been in touch with a firm she knew in Blackburn and ordered gingham dresses in blue and white check and white aprons with a bib, the correct uniform for a nursemaid. Sheena had mentioned it was to be Maria who had been a maid at the house near Kyrenia. Jenny judged her to be a size twelve.

The daily cleaning woman, Mrs Blick, was engaged for longer hours and she, with Mrs Sproson's help, began cleaning and restoring the nursery suite and rooms with bathrooms nearby for Sheena and the young Cypriot boy.

When she left on her journey, having told Nikita the day and time of her arrival, Jenny took only a small case for herself with cotton clothes, for it was still warm in Cyprus in the month of September, and also a sweater or two for possible chilly evenings. The big case contained all the gifts she had collected for the Josephides family and Tante Helena.

She felt sure Sheena would accept her invitation, leaving Nikita to his complicated business endeavours – about the young boy, Jenny did not allow herself to count on seeing him. She could only hope and pray.

As far as she knew Sheena and Nikita's baby son had not yet been christened, but no doubt all would be made clear to her when she reached the island.

She had previously mentioned the idea of adopting a war orphan to Jonathan who promised to speak to a man he knew at the Home Office. He thought there would be no difficulty in adopting a war orphan.

He had already made preliminary enquiries and she was delighted to hear that there should be no great obstacles although she knew she must not build her own hopes too high. All depended on the boy's mother.

The daily gardener, who was able to drive and had a current licence, was warned that she may be bringing several people back from Cyprus with her and she may have to ask him to drive her car to Heathrow to meet her party and help with luggage. Her son would let him know details in due course.

Jonathan took her to Heathrow to see her off and wish her luck. The flight took a bit longer than flying to Nicosia, but was otherwise comfortable and on time.

Nikita, looking decidedly thinner, was there to meet her and drove her to her hotel in Limassol to deposit her case and register. They had a drink and a sandwich in the bar and then set off for the coast road drive to Paphos. The south of the island had none of the natural beauty of the north.

Jenny asked about Nikita's new business interests and was told things were proceeding exceedingly well. He would soon have a splendid new house for his family and he had architects working on plans for a large hotel to attract foreign visitors.

Jenny explained that she wanted to send money to him to his box number from her Swiss bank. This was for Spiros' widow. He would perhaps advise her how to spend it wisely. This he gladly agreed to do.

A while later when she began to broach the subject of adopting one of Spiros' sons, he frowned silently and said she might find Christella difficult to persuade. It was entirely up to Jenny herself to point out the advantages for the child's future. There should be no difficulty in getting an exit permit for the child under present circumstances. He would of course be glad to help her.

At the hotel in Paphos, Sheena appeared looking fatter than ever but tearfully glad to see her and the baby George was a miniature Nikita. Young Maria, who Jenny recognised as having been a housemaid at their home near Kyrenia, although shy, was pleased to see her and obviously enjoying her promotion. After a while she took Master George away and left the adults to talk in peace.

When Jenny issued her invitation to go back to England with her where a complete nursery suite awaited them, Sheena at once said she would be delighted to go, leaving Nikita to get on with his many tasks. Nikita also agreed it was a good idea and Sheena said it was simply a matter of getting a passport for Maria. George could be entered on Sheena's passport.

After many lurid descriptions of the Turkish invasion had been recounted, Jenny hesitantly mentioned her wish to adopt one of the Josephides boys. Sheena looked doubtful but said Nikita would explain all the advantages her second son was being offered and especially that he may grow up to become a naval officer. On the strength of Nikita's advice, Christella may well agree.

It was arranged that Nikita drive Jenny back to the Appolonia Hotel and that she should get them to hire a car for her which she would drive over to Paphos as soon as possible.

Meanwhile, Sheena would let Tante Helena know of Jenny's impending visit. After one more glance at the baby, Nikita and Jenny set off for Limassol.

The car-hire representative at the hotel said he could provide a small Renault the next day, and Jenny duly signed the necessary papers and gave the man a cheque.

After dinner that evening, after waving Nikita off she went down through the pleasant gardens to the beach. This was quite pleasant in its way, but there was nothing of the charm of the northern coastline about the place.

Her room was comfortable enough and, after a light meal, she went to bed and slept better than on many previous nights, but before she dropped off to sleep, she prayed that Christella would be amenable, and she tried to remember exactly what little Mandis looked like. It was only the eyes she remembered clearly – those rare strange light gold eyes with the dark-ringed iris. She drifted off into a dreamless sleep.

The next day a small red car was delivered to her at the hotel. She was assured that the tank was full of petrol and the engine in perfect order.

She set off for Paphos about eleven o'clock and arrived at the hotel to be greeted enthusiastically by Sheena who said she had been thinking deeply about her generous invitation, and was much looking forward to be going to Jenny's house. They looked in at Maria who was rocking George to sleep and retreated softly to have lunch in the dining room.

'How do you keep so slim?' Sheena asked Jenny.

'I was thin for a while but am now gaining weight again,' Jenny told her.

'I must go on a diet once the baby is weaned,' Sheena said, and Jenny assured her she would help her diet and enrol her at a club in Beaconsfield where she could do aerobics and have good massage.

Sheena was very grateful and told Jenny that Nikita would be joining them after lunch to make the auspicious visit to Christella and Tante Helena.

The meeting in the old warehouse did not go quite as smoothly as Jenny would have wished. Christella thanked Jenny humbly and charmingly for all her gifts, but did not understand why she wanted to adopt Mandis who was not nearly so strong and healthy as her eldest son Kahn.

At this point Nikita stepped in and said the younger boy needed more care and attention than burly Kahn and this was a heaven-sent opportunity for him to become strong and well and under Jenny's care – -he may even grow up to be a fine naval officer of whom she would be proud.

Tante Helena seconded Nikita's reasoning and at last, somewhat tearfully, Christella agreed. Seeing the woman's tears Jenny experienced a wave of guilt and almost broke down, but Nikita was keeping a close eye on the negotiations and silenced her. Chocolates were handed round and Tante Helena made them coffee. All the children clung closely round their Mother and Jenny silently called herself a bitch and felt self-disgust for a moment. Nikita hinted there would be visits and that they would all be meeting up from time to time.

Meanwhile Christella had a sound income from now on from Mrs Lander and had quite enough to do to bring up the rest of her family.

Nikita said that his wife, baby son, Maria, Mrs Lander and Mandis all expected to leave in about one week's time. Mrs Lander would write often to him to give updates on her son's progress and he himself would come and translate the messages to her. Christella began to smile through her tears, and she got up and crossed the floor and held out her work-stained hand to Jenny who quickly grasped it in her own. In a simple gesture the woman kissed Jenny's hand and smiled her thanks and bowed, then resumed her seat among the youngsters. Jenny looked at Mandis and could see Spiros in his face and suppressed her tears.

In French, Tante Helena assured Jenny that everything would work out the way she wanted and gave Jenny her blessing.

They trooped out of the building and Sheena put an arm round Jenny's shoulders and told her she was doing a wonderful thing. Back at their hotel Jenny explained to Nikita her plan to send Mandis first to a private school where he would have some simple individual tuition in English and then when ready he would be sent to Pangbourne, a fine introduction to a naval career. The boy may eventually end up with a commission in the Merchant Navy.

Meanwhile, he would have as a family friend her own grandson, just a couple of years older than Mandis. If at first he felt homesick, he could always turn to Maria. It would be a happy household. Tante Helena would no doubt keep an eye on the rest of the Josephides family and a brighter future lay ahead for all of them. Nikita agreed.

Maria was sent for and told the arrangements and said she would of course have to ask permission from her family to leave the island, but had no doubt that they would agree it was a good opportunity for her. She was told to bring baby George down for them all to see and she hastened to fetch the sleeping child. Even asleep he looked the image of his Father and Nikita's pride was obvious to all.

Sheena accepted the big empty suitcase which had contained all the presents for the Josephides family and next day started on her own packing. Maria went to see her own family, who were camping in a tent in one of the orange groves, and received their whole-hearted approval of her future life.

Jenny spent days on the beach, visiting her Paphos friends on alternate days until at last they all pronounced themselves ready to leave on their big adventure.

Maria and Mandis had of course never flown before and were very shaky and nervous, but once airborne settled down to enjoy the experience.

On seeing them off, Nikita had hugged Jenny very closely, and she didn't, for once, withdraw from his embrace. They were indeed very good friends now and trusted each other. He swore that when a house had been built and he had some business working he would be coming over to England to fetch his family. Maria let Mandis cling onto her arm until they were all safely abroad.

Four hours or so later they were landing at Heathrow and, after a short delay in Immigration, their passports and various papers were stamped. Luggage was collected from the carousel and loaded onto a trolley, and Jenny was immensely relieved to see Jonna waving at them at the barrier.

They all piled into his big Mercedes and Jenny's gardener stood by to pack the baggage into her car.

It was an enormous relief to be back at Foresters and find Mrs Sproson ready to welcome them all. She had arranged a meal on the kitchen table and Jenny was pleased to see Jonna had brought Timmy over. The two young boys eyed each other warily but after the meal Jenny was delighted to see them running around the garden with Ben. They would gradually find their own means of communication.

Sheena and Maria were very impressed by the lovely nursery suite and their adjacent rooms. Poor little Mandis seemed stunned by the whole thing, but Tim took him and showed him the room he was to have and how all the taps worked in the bathroom.

After Maria had put George to bed in the pretty cot, she volunteered to look after Mandis and, after getting him to say thank you to Jenny and Mrs Sproson, took him up and put him to bed in his own room. She sat with him until he fell asleep.

Sheena and Jenny sat in the drawing room having a glass of pale sherry and Maria shyly sort out Mrs Sproson in the big kitchen.

She was introduced to little Ming and was pleased when the cat settled down on her lap and purred. Presently Mrs Sproson gave the girl some peas to shell and put into a colander and with smiles and gestures and Maria's few words of English they got on well enough.

When Jenny came into the room she asked Maria if she liked her own bedroom, but the girl did not seem to understand, so Jenny led her up to it and showed her where she could put her own things. The girl did her unpacking in a matter of five minutes and was delighted when Jenny produced her new nurse's uniform. The sizes were right and the girl hurried to show her new things to her mistress. Sheena was pleased too. Jenny assured them both that, for the winter, she would be provided with much warmer dresses to wear under her starched aprons.

Jenny suggested that on their first evening they would eat in the kitchen with Mrs Sproson, but usually she and Sheena would have their main meals in the dining room.

SEVENTEEN

Mandis spoke a few words and phrases in English. Maria, who was slightly more fluent, haltingly explained that Mandis had done well at the infants' school he had been attending in Paphos.

A few days later Jenny went down to the village junior school and sought the advice of the Headmaster. He advised her to send the boy to a nearby private junior school where, if she cared to pay for it, the boy could have individual tuition. Jenny hastened to do this and, when the next term started, it had been arranged that Mandis should start his private coaching there.

At first he seemed alarmed at yet another new adventure, but when his tutor turned out to be an eighteen-year-old student filling in time until he went up to university, he relaxed and settled in easily. The hours of tuition were relieved with games or play time and each day Jenny was delighted to see that the boy was happily settled into his new routine.

He still seemed more attached to Maria than to herself, but Jenny decided on the drives backwards and forwards to school he would gradually become closer to her.

One day she realised the boy would probably like a bicycle, so she went straight into the town and bought two – one for herself and another for a seven- or eight-year-old. The next time Tim was home from school she invited him over and, after having relearned how to ride herself, asked her grandson to help Mandis.

At first the child was very shaky, but with help from herself, was now quite proficient. Mandis soon got past the nervous wobbly stage and sailed off confidently round the lawn with a smile on his face.

The two boys played happily together with the new cycles. Of course there were the usual grazed knees and skinned fingers but these were dealt with by Mrs Sproson and progress was rapidly made. Jenny took many photos of Mandis to send home to his family. The boy was especially pleased to see these.

At his school Mandis found there were children of various nationalities so did not feel especially strange and applied himself to his work with his pleasant new tutor with eagerness.

Meanwhile, Jenny had rung up and made an appointment to see the Bursar at Pangbourne College. She was told the boy would receive a semi-nautical training, starting in the junior school at eight, and could progress to the senior part at twelve. This would carry on until the age of eighteen when he would have the necessary qualifications to apply for a job with the Merchant Navy.

This all sounded ideal. She was a little worried about his health and stamina but, taking him to her own doctor, was assured that the boy was in perfect health and would gradually gain weight as he became used to his new diet.

When Jenny tried to commiserate with Sheena about her husband's losses in the north of Cyprus, Sheena laughingly told her that Nikita had plenty of money stacked away and, in any case, would be into making another fortune from his new plans in the south. He had, Sheena said, the Midas touch.

Sheena was truly delighted with the smart nursery suite at her disposal and was soon seeking Mrs Sproson's help on the subject of weaning. Thin oats porridge plus various small jars from the supermarket were prescribed and the young George was soon taking solid food.

Maria was thrilled by her nursemaid's uniform and the pleasure of her very own room and thanked Jenny frequently. Jenny took pictures of the girl to send to her own family – that is to say, through Nikita's box number.

Sheena was enrolled at a local health club and was enrolled on a series of slimming exercises and, given a diet sheet, had gradually begun to resume her normal young figure.

Sometimes Jenny and her sister-in-law went off on bicycle rides together and they both grew healthier as the weeks went by.

Sad news came from Paphos that Tante Helena had died after an attack of pneumonia. Jenny and Sheena asked Nikita to order special floral wreaths for her funeral and Sheena wrote a special note to Christella to try to comfort her.

Two or three trips into Beaconsfield were necessary to buy Sheena some smart new clothes for her new, slimmer figure, and a good hairdresser also helped the young woman's appearance.

While driving Mandis to and from school, Jenny always hoped the boy would talk to her – even confide – but he just stared out of the windows and remained silent. Going home, if he had a special drawing or piece of work for which he had received praise, it was to Mrs Sproson he rushed to show it. This hurt Jenny very much but she told herself it was only a matter of time. She must be patient.

A note brought home from the school one day announced Sports Day would be on the following Saturday. Jenny asked Jonathan if he would come and support her. He seemed to understand her concern and agreed to do so.

This was the day when that special talent, which in her innermost heart Jenny was sure the boy possessed, manifested itself. He could run very, very fast, barefoot. In the hundred yards race he won by several feet competing with taller, more muscular boys than himself. He was awarded the cup: a tawdry E.P.N.S. copy of a larger silver cup, but on which his year and name would be duly inscribed.

After this race, poor little Mandis seemed exhausted and Jenny suggested they should leave. Jonathan drove and Jenny sat in the back cuddling Mandis for the first time.

She felt nothing in life had been worth anything before, as though any emotion she had ever known – not even the height of sexual passion – could compare with this.

When they got to the house, Jonathan lifted the boy and carried him up to his bed. He was now deeply asleep. Jenny carefully took off his shoes and smoothed his pillow and pulled the duvet up to his chin. Taking the precious little cup, she put it on his bedside table and sat with him for a long time as he slept.

The old house seemed full and alive again these days. Although Mrs Sproson, now well over eighty, was as energetic and cheerful as ever, her once mouse-brown hair was now snow-white but still scraped up in a bun on the crown of her head.

Jenny had taken good care of Mrs Sproson's health, taking her to Jenny's own dentist and doctor and a first class optician for reading glasses. These she chose herself. Plain gold-rimmed no-nonsense ones.

The daily gardener, Joe, could drive and kept up his licence so that from time to time he could leave Jenny free to take Sheena up to London and do the school run for her.

So far, a name had not been chosen for Nikita's son, but one day Sheena told her she had received a letter telling her Nikita had decided to call the boy George Nikita and he should be christened at a Greek Orthodox church when his Father came to take the family home to their grand new house.

Jenny prepared herself to put on a special party for this event but it was not to be for some considerable time yet.

Jenny, by appointment, took Mandis over to Pangbourne College one day and the boy was fascinated by the boys in their semi-nautical navy uniforms, and was very impressed by the place. Jenny assured the Bursar that the boy's English was improving rapidly and that he showed no difficulty over most subjects. She also mentioned his athletic prowess which especially interested and impressed the Bursar.

'He will be playing rugby in the senior school here,' he told her, 'so he should be very popular.'

So, his name was formally entered for both junior and senior schools and she took away a syllabus and fees chart and, as an afterthought, a clothes and equipment list.

She took countless photographs of Sheena and the baby and sent them off to Nikita, then took many of Mandis with Timothy or alone with his bicycle, which she sent to Nikita to hand over to Christella.

Not long after this came news that Christella had remarried – a man who worked in Nikita's factory. No doubt she was counted a well-off widow.

It was a happy household, and the children loved the animals and the freedom of the large garden and paddock in which to play. Timothy and Mandis became firm friends and Mrs Sproson was the great matriarchal figure to them all.

Jenny was pleased to realise when she was fitting up a desk for Mandis in his room that a number of Myles' things bore the same initials as the child who gradually inherited blotter, hair brushes, address book and luggage. She saved Myles' briefcase until the child was grown up.

After hearing of Christella's remarriage, Jenny no longer spent sleepless nights reminding herself she had stolen the boy. Christella would probably have several more.

Gradually Mandis grew closer to Jenny and would sometimes lean near her and tell her of his own secret ambitions. He wanted to become a first rate athlete and play games well, and then he wanted to become a sailor like his Father. So, she had done all the right things for him.

When she took him to have his small cup engraved, he reached up and kissed her cheek and sometimes, when she saw him into bed, he would beg her to stay and tell him a story. It was a repetition of her relationship with Jonna only now she knew that all too soon the intimate affection must stop.

When young George was nearly three, Nikita announced his imminent arrival and a flurry of activity surged through the place. A Greek church had to be found and a christening party arranged.

The church was located in Reading and the formalities negotiated. Mrs Sproson made a magnificent cake. George was put into shoes for the first time and everyone had a new outfit for the occasion.

Jenny went to Heathrow to meet Nikita and found him much thinner and considerably older. He had a mountain of luggage and, on the way back, told Jenny he had built a fine house for his family and a spacious new hotel to attract foreign visitors. His citrus industry was established and a factory had been built. He thanked her volubly for all she had done for his wife and son and said she must consider bringing her own family out to Paphos for a holiday soon after he had got his own family settled.

He was duly impressed with Foresters and Jenny's lavish decor and asked about her adopted son. Jenny said he must soon judge for himself, but told him of her plans for the naval school and also of his athletic skills. Nikita was impressed.

The reunion of Sheena, baby George and Nikita was very moving and the news that plans had been made for the christening delighted him. He said he would buy the champagne and urged Jenny to be sure and invite some of her friends and family.

As he had asked, she fixed the date, and invited Jonna, Gayle and the children and, on impulse, Lulu and her husband and Filly, newly married to an airline pilot.

The occasion was on a Sunday, so everyone turned up looking very smart. Lulu was drenched in a new scent strong enough to knock out a horse, but Nikita was attracted to her nevertheless.

The ceremony went off well, with young George Nikita yelling loudly when doused with the holy water, but once back at the house all was noise and merriment. Young Maria and Mrs Sproson were invited to join in the celebrations and the entertainment went on until late evening. Many, many photographs were taken and when Nikita spoke in Greek to Mandis, the boy had some difficulty in replying. He ran to Jenny who put an arm round him and told him not to worry. English was his first language now.

At last the happy Greek family retired to their rooms and Jenny put Mandis to bed and stayed until he dropped off to sleep.

Late in the evening, after some of the debris had been cleared and the animals fed, Mrs Sproson and Jenny sat at the kitchen table and talked over the party. The old woman was pleased all had gone so well and confessed she now felt very, very tired.

'I think our Greek visitors will be going back to Cyprus very soon and life will be quieter for us,' Jenny said. 'You go off to bed and I will do breakfast in the morning so you can have a lie-in.'

The old woman went off with old Ben trailing after her and peace reigned once more. Jenny picked up sleepy Ming and went slowly up to her own room.

EIGHTEEN

The year was 1985. Mrs Sproson had died in her sleep the previous winter and Ben had stopped eating and died a few days later. Ming, who was very old and shaky, was found by Jenny curled up stiff and lifeless in the lavender bed a week or so later.

Both animals were buried under the walnut tree in the orchard. Jenny wept as she shovelled the final spadeful of earth into the grave and threw in flowers and some of Ming's favourite cat-mint and Valerian.

The next autumn the old tree, which had not born walnuts for several years, was weighed down with a bumper crop. This made Jenny determined to state in her will that she wished to be buried and not cremated. She liked to think her old body, when the time came, would enrich the ground and make something grow.

To replace Mrs Sproson she had answered an advertisement in the *Telegraph* which read, 'Young French chef seeks job with family in England to improve English.' From the Box number she received an interesting reply to her own letter and wrote again engaging the student. He was only two years older than Mandis but he came from a family restaurant background and intended later to go to a hotel-training school in Switzerland, and it was important that he improve his English.

His name was Didier, and he sent Jenny his flight number and date of arrival and she went to meet him at Heathrow. He was short for his age, dark, with rather too much hair and very little English, but once installed and let loose in the kitchen proved he could cook. All his French dishes were excellent and he was keen to try to make any English food Jenny suggested. They spent many mornings laughingly producing simple English recipes like shepherds pie and roast beef and Yorkshire pudding, and the inevitable trifle. He did not approve of Bird's custard, but as all her family liked it, it had to be learned.

One sunny morning Jenny sat in the Orangerie reflecting on the amazing metamorphosis that had happened to Mandis.

At seventeen he was six feet tall, slim, but well muscled in the right places. He had done well academically, was an athlete and a great games player.

Best of all was his astonishing sense of humour. His English had no trace of accent and he was affectionate and made her laugh much of the time they were together.

In his navy cadet's uniform with the gold buttons and various added insignia he was a most attractive looking young man with his Father's extraordinary eyes. She loved him very much.

The first time he met Didier he greeted the young Frenchman in his own language until Jenny told him he must always speak in English, as Didier was only in England to improve his poor knowledge of the language. This he agreed to do and somehow they seemed to get along very well.

Sitting with an arm round her shoulders in her favourite spot in the Orangerie one morning, she told Mandis of her plan to take her whole family out to Cyprus for a holiday. His face clouded over momentarily and this worried Jenny. Perhaps he didn't want to go back to his origins. She questioned this and he quickly smiled and agreed it was a great idea. She intended to take Jonathan and his family with them. Nikita could put them all up at his splendid new hotel. But, Jenny assured him, if the idea didn't really please him she would forget the whole thing. Mandis hastened to impress on her that he had had only fleeting doubts and finally decided the trip would be great fun. He hugged her impulsively and then jumped up and said he must change into some old clothes. He was only home for the day and must be back at Pangbourne before eight o'clock in the evening. He had taken a bus part of the way to get home and hitched a lift for the last bit.

So, after telling Didier they would have soup and cheese omelettes for lunch and anything he liked to concoct for dessert, she hastened to ring up Jonathan at his office.

Fortunately he wasn't too busy to talk to her, and when she told him of the proposed trip as soon as the school holidays started and Tim was home from Oxford, he immediately accepted the invitation and said he thought they would all enjoy it. He would of course have to consult Gayle first, but he was pretty sure she would welcome a holiday.

Jonna rang her back late in the evening and confirmed that Gayle heartily approved and so Jenny could write to Sheena and as soon as a reply was forthcoming, could book all the tickets.

Sheena's reply was rather late in coming, but at last her letter arrived saying they were all delighted and would book them in for whatever dates Jenny would like.

She wrote again saying 20 July for three weeks. It would, of course, be very hot in Paphos in the middle of the Summer, but so far there had been very little sun in England that year and they could all do with some.

Telling Didier of her plans, she suggested he may like to invite a friend over to stay with him while they were away, and he was quite excited by the suggestion.

Jenny took the precaution of having a word with old Joe the gardener, asking him to keep an eye on the place and if she left her telephone number in Paphos, he could ring her if anything was wrong. She also asked Lulu to look in from time to time while she was away.

Lulu was glad to help and said if she went away, Filly, who lived quite close in the neighbourhood, would check up in her place.

As soon as the confirmation of accommodation was received from Cyprus, Jenny booked flights.

They were a party of six. All in light holiday clothes, the four-and-a-half-hour flight was filled with jokes and hilarity. Nikita was at Larnaca to meet them with two big cars. A much thinner Nikita, now showing stress lines and a touch of grey in his hair.

Sheena and little George were waiting for them on the verandah of the hotel. Sheena had put on weight again and on a double take, Jenny realised she was pregnant again.

When they had all been shown their rooms and had their suitcases collected, they were offered iced drinks in an air conditioned bar. Nikita could hardly take his eyes off Mandis and quietly congratulated Jenny on her wonderful upbringing of the boy.

'Should I send him alone to see his Mother?' she asked Nikita.

'No. You take him there yourself. He is no longer Greek. He needs you. Tomorrow will be time enough.'

For dinner they were invited to Nikita and Sheena's fine new villa. It turned out to be half a mile from the hotel and was an even bigger white palace than the one in Kyrenia. The furnishings were perhaps not quite so grand, but opulent enough, and came mostly from Europe. Some even from Harrods.

They had the same but now much older cook and the food was delectable. The main rooms had huge fans despite the fact that the bedrooms were air conditioned.

After dinner, during which a lot of the pale golden wine was drunk, Mandis asked Jenny when should he go to see his Father's family. It struck her as odd that he had said 'his Father's family' and made no mention of his Mother.

'Tomorrow, darling, and I will go with you. We will take them all the presents I have bought for them. Don't be nervous.'

'I wish I didn't have to go!' he whispered to her and reached for her hand.

'Silly boy. I am your Mother now,' she said.

After dinner, when the sun had gone down, it was blissfully cooler. Some of them stayed in and played backgammon and others, including Jenny, Mandis and Fleur, who surprisingly had grown into a quite shy slim girl, went for a walk down to the shore. Mandis was very quiet and stayed close to Jenny, which worried her. Perhaps it had been a mistake to bring him back to his early environment.

When darkness fell they all decided to go back to their hotel. Nikita drove them in relays.

In Jenny's room Mandis helped her sort out all the presents she had brought for Christella and the children. They were mostly clothes and, for the girls, pretty watches and beads and, of course, boxes of chocolates.

'Go to bed now, darling – we could all do with some sleep. I'll see you for breakfast at eight-thirty and we'll decide when to go to see Christella and her family.'

Mandis kissed her cheek and thanked her. He seemed oddly depressed and loathe to leave her, and she began to worry again about the wisdom of bringing the boy back to his early background.

She was very tired and, after a cool shower, was glad to get into bed with a book which soon fell from her hands. As soon as she had switched off the light she fell fast asleep.

She did not wake until a maid knocked at her door and came in with a tray of tea things. Another knock and Mandis came in and, fetching a tooth mug from the bathroom, shared her tea with her. He seemed more cheerful and Jenny reminded him they would have to ring Nikita to take them to the place the Josephides were now living.

'Put on your uniform, please, Mandis. It would please Christella to see you have grown up to be a real sailor, that's why I asked you to bring it,' Jenny said gently.

'Rather idiotic, but if it pleases you, OK,' he said, and went back to his own room.

She rang Nikita's house number and he told her he would be picking her and Mandis up at half-past ten.

As it was a Saturday, the family children should all be at home, Jenny thought, as she tied the parcels with ribbons. Mandis, in his cadet's uniform, was waiting for her on the terrace and Nikita turned up on time and they collected all the parcels and climbed into his spacious Mercedes.

A short drive along a quay brought them to the big warehouse. The ground floor had indeed been made pleasantly habitable. Although it was open-space living, they seemed to have everything necessary. Christella, also heavily pregnant, greeted them and looked shyly at Mandis who towered over her. He bent and kissed her cheek and said hello to two young girls who had been babies when he left. The parcels were handed over and there were many exclamations of thanks and delight.

Christella offered them home-made lemonade which they drank from plastic glasses and cushions were brought out for them all to sit on. In the background Jenny could see several tiers of bunk beds and, through a door at the back of the vast room, a bathroom or kitchen. Certainly they had running water. She hoped there was an indoor toilet and a bath. Nikita translated everything Jenny had to say and, for Jenny's benefit, all Christella's effusive thanks and her admiration of Mandis. He was a true sailor now and would soon have a job on a ship, Nikita told her, and at this she shed tears, but they were tears of joy.

Mandis was getting restless and Jenny felt much sympathy for him, so she decided to cut short the visit. Nikita was fully in agreement and they

117

all kissed and bowed and hurried back into Nikita's car.

'I hope Christella's husband is a good man,' Jenny said.

Nikita told her he was one of his best workers.

'Can we swim? Is there a good beach near?' Mandis asked and, hearing that the sea was ideal for swimming, asked if they had time to go for a bathe. Jenny smiled, and asked Nikita to drive them back to the hotel to get their swim suits and towels and to collect any of the rest of the party who wanted to swim.

There was an excellent sandy beach not far from the hotel and it was soothing to walk into the crested waves and swim out to where the water looked turquoise. Mandis was by far the strongest swimmer and it was clear that Fleur was very attracted to him. He, on the other hand, seemed hardly aware of her presence. Gayle, who had smothered herself in sun tan oil was happy to lie on her towel on the beach. Jenny and Jonna swam out quite a long way side by side. Nikita stayed and watched the scene for a while then, declaring he didn't care for swimming, offered to come back for them in an hour.

The next day, Nikita lent them a car and they had a picnic packed by the hotel kitchen staff and drove off up country.

Then there was the visit to the famous mosaics and the recounting of the fable of Aphrodite rising from the waves. Each evening they dined with Nikita and Sheena and Nikita taught them all to dance the Zorba steps. This was fun and the young things tried and tried until they had it perfectly and poor Nikita was quite worn out.

'There is no need to visit the Josephides again – you would never remember Christella's new husband's name if I told you,' Nikita advised. 'Mandis is your son and an Englishman by now,' he advised Jenny. 'You are disturbing the boy. Leave well alone.'

One day Nikita took all the male members of the party out in a small yacht and they caught several fish and seemed to have had a great time. But Mandis was always so happy to be back with Jenny. Looking into his Father's eyes Jenny always felt tears pricking the back of her own and loved him more and more.

From the hotel Jenny rang Foresters, and, after some delay in getting through, Didier answered in English and assured her everything was in good order and asked the date of her return. She told him and he lapsed into French and said he would prepare a special dinner party for the family's return.

It was amazing how quickly the days passed with swimming, or lazing in the sun or picnics at different places along the coast. They all got very brown except Jenny, who always wore a shady straw hat to protect her fair skin. Gayle looked like a Pakistani, her husband told her.

One day they drove into Limassol where there was a big shopping centre, and Gayle bought some batik type loose kaftans and a sort of belly-dancer's outfit which they all shrieked over. Jenny bought some animal shapes carved out of garnet, and some pottery saved from the kilns in the north at the time of the Turkish invasion.

Limassol was full of Lebanese who had left their troubled city. Jenny noticed several very large warships lying a long way out to sea and was told that they were Russian and American. It seemed that the little island of Cyprus was the very centre of what could become an even more serious war involving the Middle Eastern countries.

One day Nikita drove some of them down to the great RAF base at Akrotiri where his son had been born. It was an enormous, impressive spread and Jenny felt very proud to be British.

She felt very sad that they couldn't go to the north, which was so much more beautiful, or even Nicosia which was a fascinating town. Nikita said he didn't think he could ever hope to return in his lifetime but he had high hopes for his son or sons. He would also have liked to take them up to the Troodos mountains where one could ski at certain times of the year in the morning and descend to the beach and swim the same day. It was no good crying over spilt milk, he said. Justice would triumph in the end but meanwhile, one had to get on with life as well as one could.

Driving them round his newly-planted citrus groves he proudly said would be in full production within two years. Meanwhile, his big holiday hotel was doing splendid business.

Several evenings when they stayed at the hotel for dinner instead of going to Sheena and Nikita, they were regaled with a floorshow – the inevitable Zorba dances and some much less impressive women's dances.

One night there was an English woman singer and a man playing the piano. They were not very good and performed songs from the fifties and sixties so the younger members of the party were very bored, but Jenny quite enjoyed them.

On their last night Nikita and Sheena put on a very special dinner for them and Nikita, who had a booming tenor voice, sang them some sad and some not so sad songs. He then surprised them all by producing a strange instrument called a bazouki and playing some Zorba rhythm notes on it. It was fascinating. How I have underestimated this man, Jenny reflected. He played a couple more tunes and then threw the instrument down exhausted.

They all murmured their admiration and thanks for a jolly evening and piled into their borrowed car and drove back to the hotel.

On their last evening with Sheena and Nikita, Jenny happened to mention what a pity it was they couldn't have been up to the Troodos Mountains and to her surprise Sheena said there was no reason for not going. The best way was by a road from Limassol and half way up there was a lovely hotel at Platrus where they could lunch. She added, 'Nikita only put you off going because he doesn't want his precious new car damaged by the bad roads.'

So Nikita still had his devious tendencies, Jenny thought to herself. But next time she came to Cyprus she vowed to herself she would drive up to the mountains in a hired car and also visit the famous hotel at Platrus.

Taking their seats on the aircraft, she noticed that Fleur was trying very hard to get a seat near Mandis. The girl still had those blackcurrant eyes rather too close together but was otherwise quite attractive, if still selfish. Timothy, on the other hand, although now fully grown, had the same rather diffident manner he had had as a child. Although he had been reading PPE at Oxford he intended getting himself a job with a clever young designer called Conran in London and continuing the design of clothes. Jonathan was looking decidedly middle-aged and Gayle spent most of her time keeping herself thin and attractive. She wore too much make-up and spent a great deal of money on clothes.

Jenny grabbed two seats on the starboard side of the aircraft for herself and Mandis so Fleur's efforts were wasted, but the general ambience on the flight was as jolly as the one on their way out and they arrived to find Joe had brought Jenny's car to meet them and they waited while Jonathan retrieved his car from the longterm garage space, before bidding each other goodbye.

Jenny and Mandis sat in the back of her car and Joe recounted various incidents that had happened at the house while they had been away. Didier and his friend had had a party and one window in the kitchen had been broken but quickly mended. They had not used the other parts of the house and Didier was a very reliable character. He was now alone again and preparing them a gala dinner for their return. He had charged Jenny's accounts at the butcher and grocer for this food only. Any food consumed during his friend's stay, he had paid for himself.

Jenny was naturally pleased to hear this and planned to give Didier a handsome reward when the time came for him to return to Paris.

Mandis said it was time he took driving lessons as he would like to get his licence before getting a job and Jenny assured him she would arrange all this for his next holiday period.

The boy squeezed her hand in gratitude and kissed her cheek. She considered herself lucky to have such an appreciative son and told him so. She already dreaded the day when he would go off to sea but knew she must not let him be aware of this.

Back at Foresters, after greeting Didier warmly, they went up to their rooms to bathe and change. Joe took care of their luggage.

Early in the evening they met up with Didier again in the drawing room where the young Frenchman had placed a tray with drinks and an ice bucket. Jenny mixed a dry martini which Myles had taught her to make, and they all happily toasted each other and she invited Didier to eat with them in the dining room as it was a special occasion.

He had cooked for them a delicious Vichyssoise soup, followed by Boeuf en croute with baby new potatoes and creamed spinach. For dessert he had timed a superb lemon soufflé.

After a saunter round the garden and a cursory glance at her post, they agreed an early night was a good idea.

Jenny went happily to bed knowing she still had Mandis at home for several more weeks before his last term at Pangbourne started. She would organise driving lessons for him and, after passing his test, she would give him his own car. She sank into a happy sleep.

Waking early the next morning she put out a hand for her little cat then realised he was no longer alive. She made up her mind to get another

Siamese. She would ring the cattery from which he came and order a new one. He should be called T'ang. Suddenly she realised just how much she needed the comfort of a cat on her bed. She determined to make the call – she would ring immediately after breakfast.

NINETEEN

Later next morning Jenny rang Lulu to thank her for looking in at the house during her absence and to ask her the telephone number of the driving school where Filly had been taught to drive. Lulu looked it up and gave it to her straight away.

Jenny rang the firm and asked if she could book her son in as quickly as possible for a course. To her surprise they were able to take him right away, so she booked a lesson each day for the remaining period of Mandis' holiday. Next she rang the local council offices and asked where she should apply for her son's driving test. She was given a number to ring and booked the test for the last day of his holiday.

She told Mandis he was to start driving lessons that very afternoon but did not tell him she had booked a date for his test. Mandis was very pleased.

At two o'clock she drove her own car to a position in front of the house in position for driving out of the drive.

After watching the instructor arrive as a passenger in another car, she continued to gaze at them out of the window. Mandis was in the driving seat, which had had to be pushed back a long way for his length of leg and the instructor was obviously giving her son basic first actions. Large red L plates had been fixed on the car back and front and at a very slow pace she saw the car turn down the drive onto the road. She crossed her fingers and said a silent little prayer.

While they were out she couldn't settle down to any of the household jobs she intended to do, and simply relaxed on the big sofa in the drawing room remembering Mandis in his younger days.

Early on he had developed an infectious sense of humour. She recalled how he had found an old record from a film called The Lady and the

Tramp in which there were some Siamese cats who joined in a song called, 'We are Siamese if you please', and, finding an old wind-up portable gramophone which Jonathan had owned when at school, had played the record. Then he had hunted and found little Ming and sat him down on a cushion nearby. When the song ended, the cats on the record, or whoever was imitating them, miaowed loudly and Ming, hearing this, joined in. He had put on the record several times and when the song 'We are Siamese if you please' came on, he tapped Ming gently on his head and he miaowed in unison. He rehearsed this until the little cat got it right every time and then called Jenny in to listen. It was very funny to hear and see, and Ming seemed to enjoy his performance. Jenny laughed until she cried.

He was forever bringing home jokes from school, some of them a little blue for his Mother's taste but always funny. He made up a lot of his own and learned to play a guitar reasonably well. When asked if he would like tuition he had turned down her offer flat, saying this was just a passing amusement. He would rather learn another language. Japanese perhaps? This notion did not ever come to anything, as by this time all he had time for was rowing or learning navigation.

She was relieved when she saw her car returning with Mandis at the wheel, and ran outside to hear what the instructor had to say. He said Mandis showed really good ability and already had a sound road sense. He reckoned that by the end of the holidays he would be driving competently and ready for his test.

Jenny thanked the middle-aged man, and offered to drive him back to the driving school. He said there was no need. He had already arranged to be picked up. A white Metro came up the drive as he finished explaining, and a second lesson was agreed for the next day.

Mandis told her the whole thing was much easier than he had thought, and he already felt quite competent. She, however, insisted that he must finish the course.

They went into the house with their arms around each other and drank orange juice in the kitchen with Didier.

In the afternoon she took him in to Reading to a cinema to see 'The Sting', a classic film which she had seen before but he had not. Mandis enjoyed it as much as she did and they giggled all the way home.

The driving lessons continued confidently and Jenny knew that her son would be well up to his test just before his return to school.

One day she rang up her grandson Tim and invited him to a theatre in London with Mandis, a few evenings before the boy was due back at school. She chose a comedy with Richard Briers in the lead and they all enjoyed it very much. Afterwards they all had supper at a rather noisy restaurant in the King's Road which was full of people their own age rather than hers. The food was definitely junk but the boys liked it which was all that mattered.

Taking a taxi back to the garage off Piccadilly where she had parked her car, they paid the costly bill and gave Tim a lift home to Barnes and then drove back to the A40 where traffic was heavy and fast. Mandis begged to be allowed to drive but she adamantly refused to let him.

'Only when you have passed your test and have your licence,' she told him.

He did not ask again and next time she glanced at him saw that he was dozing. She was probably driving too slowly for his liking but she was always especially careful at night.

It was late when they got back home and she sent Mandis straight up to bed in order to be fit for his lesson the next day.

Jenny was now fifty-nine years old. She had managed to keep fit and weighed the same as she did at nineteen, but she knew her reflexes were slower and she had to wear glasses for reading and driving, and different ones for television.

When she went up to bed she studied herself closely in her bathroom mirror and saw there were silver-grey streaks in her blue-black hair. Her eyes were still the same brilliant blue but she knew that she would age rapidly once Mandis had finally got himself a job and gone away. She was stupid not to have kept closer to the few friends she had. She must prepare herself for old age. She was quite aware that men often took second glances at her but she could not imagine ever caring for another man. Thinking of her greying hair, she realised that we grow our own premature shroud, which in turn reminded her she still had not got around to making her will. She would do that soon.

Then what? She couldn't go on living in limbo like this, always hoping for something she wasn't sure would ever happen.

She had a bath and went to bed with a new novel but after she realised she was reading the same lines over and over again, gave up and put out the light.

The driving lessons continued well and when she told Mandis the date of the test, he smiled smugly and said, 'It's a piece of cake!'

Of course he was right, and he got his licence with a minimum of fuss. She promised him a car of his own when he had left school. Meanwhile he could drive hers when he was at home.

TWENTY

As soon as she had had breakfast the next morning, she spoke to her Swiss bank and, speaking to the manager, told him to reduce the amount he sent each month to Mr Nikita Christofides in Paphos, Cyprus to one half the amount from now on. She was told to kindly write these instructions in confirmation and her wishes would be carried out.

She wrote her letter in French and gave her account number. Next she telephoned her solicitor in Beaconsfield and asked for an appointment to make her will. She was given a time early in the afternoon.

The matter of the will proved simpler than she had anticipated. She told her competent middle-aged adviser that, on her death, she wanted to leave all her money and the house to Mandis Lander, her adopted son, except for two donations each of one thousand pounds to the RSPCA and to the World Wild Life Trust. All her jewellery was to go to Mandis's wife. She wished to be buried, not cremated, in as light as possible wooden coffin so that her remains should benefit any earth animals or nearby trees, flowers or grass. While all this was being typed on a document by a secretary, she explained that her son Jonathan had already been well looked after by her dead husband and was well-off in his own right.

The solicitor said she was very young to be making a will and when she told him her age seemed very surprised. She went on to say there was one other matter over which she would like his help. She wanted to leave a large sum of money in trust for her son Mandis when he became twenty-one. This was of course in case she should die or be killed before he reached this age. Her solicitor told her that he would have a document prepared and sent to her and, if she approved it, she could sign it and return it to him for safe keeping.

When she returned to the house, she rang Jonathan and told him simply that she had made her will which was being kept by her solicitor in Beaconsfield and gave his name, address and phone number. She did not divulge anything of the wording of the will but did inform him that she had arranged to leave twenty thousand pounds in trust for Mandis in case she should die or be killed before he reached this age.

'Highly unlikely!' was Jonna's only comment, but he agreed she was being very wise. She was grateful to Jonna for looking after all her income tax problems and also the outgoings on the house. She told him she had reduced the pension she had been paying to the Cypriot family and was not going to engage another cook once the French boy went back to Paris. It was time she did some cooking herself. Would they all like to come over for lunch next Sunday?

Jonathan accepted readily and said he looked forward to seeing her, as he did not see enough of her.

For the rest of the day she did some tidying up in the Orangerie and then, after a bath, had a drink and a light dinner with Didier in the kitchen. He had made tremendous progress over his English and they chatted away for almost two hours during which time she only needed to correct him on a few words.

She told him she hoped he would stay until Mandis had done his final exams and left Pangbourne, and he agreed to do this. He was most insistent that she and Mandis should visit him and his family in Paris, or rather in St Cloud where they had the family restaurant, and Jenny, smiling broadly, said nothing would make her happier.

She told him about her family coming over for lunch the following Sunday.

He said, 'Of course, ze Ros Bif and Yowksher poudan.'

'No,' she replied, 'give them a truly French meal. Just tell me what to buy, anything you need and I will buy the ingredients.'

They drank one more glass of wine and Jenny, tired out by the day's activities, went off to bed with her book.

The next morning her solicitor telephoned her just to check that her bank was indeed Lloyds in Beaconsfield and said he knew the manager well. She would be receiving the trust fund document to sign shortly and also a copy of her will, which she had already signed, for her to keep.

Missing Mandis very much she was wandering aimlessly round the garden when she saw out of the corner of her eye a tall shabby old man approaching the front door. He was very thin and wore a dirty old raincoat, had a thick grisly grey beard and a battered dirty old felt hat pulled down over his eyes. He looked most unsavoury.

She went diffidently towards him. To her horror he whipped round and seized her in his arms and whirled her round and round then burst out laughing. She had already caught a glimpse of those well known eyes and started laughing.

'Mandis – you idiot – put me down – what are you doing here?'

'Only one more exam to go and I just missed you so much I had to come over.'

'Come in and take off that ghastly smelly old beard and coat. You had better have a bath.'

'Don't nag. I had to walk most of the way. No lifts this time except for a lorry from Bradfield.'

'Hurry inside and up to your room – I'll run you a bath. You had better burn the old coat, hat and beard.'

'For God's sake – NO! They come from the props cupboard at school!'

'Well, no wonder you couldn't get a lift – go and show yourself to Didier in the kitchen.'

As she ran upstairs she heard Didier greeting Mandis in voluble French. He wasn't fooled for an instant but roared with laughter.

'Epatent mon copain,' she heard Didier shout.

After he had bathed and changed, she poured Mandis a cold lager and they sat on the big sofa and laughed at his silly trick.

'No, seriously – I just had to get away for a breather. Must be back before eight tonight. Tomorrow is my very last test and I'll know all the results in about three days. If I've failed I shan't come home.'

'You know you won't fail. I would bet on it!' Jenny said stroking his hair.

Didier came in and asked them what they would like for lunch.

'Sausages and mash,' Mandis said.

'Nonsense, and in any case we haven't got any sausages,' said Jenny. 'Make us something French, Didier, please,' she added and he went away smiling to himself.

'You might have given your old Mum a heart attack you know, you silly boy,' she told her son.

'Or robbed a bank,' Mandis said.

'There will be no need for that. Only yesterday I arranged for you to be given a substantial sum of money when you are twenty-one,' she told him.

'And until then if I don't get a job, I starve?' he asked, putting his head on her shoulder.

'Probably,' she said. 'I shall take you back with your horrible disguise in a plastic bag and you must get a good night's sleep

before the finals tomorrow,' she concluded firmly and poured herself a drink.

When Didier came in to say that lunch was ready, Mandis had dropped off to sleep and Jenny could see by the shadows under his eyes that he was, in fact, exhausted.

She woke him up to eat a delicious quiche Lorraine with ham and cheese and eggs and thinly-sliced green peppers in it. Afterwards came some creamy chocolate ice cream from the freezer. They all ate in the kitchen and then Mandis stretched out on the couch in the drawing room and slept for an hour.

When he woke up it was to find Jenny standing over him saying, 'I am going to run you back now. You must get an early night and be really fit and at your best tomorrow. Here are your horrible things from your precious props cupboard, in this plastic bag. I have sprayed them with deodorant. Come on, I'm going to run you back right now.'

Mandis smoothed back his hair and rubbed his eyes. 'I'll just say goodbye to Didier and be with you,' he said.

Jenny hastened to get her car out of the garage and let him take the driving seat. He drove well and cautiously and she was pleased and impressed.

They stopped at the main gates of the school and Mandis kissed and thanked her and took the plastic bag from the back seat.

She watched as he walked slowly towards a side entrance, then turned the car and made for home.

She had every conviction that he would have done well when the final verdict was announced, but felt a pang of sympathy for his coming ordeal.

TWENTY-ONE

As she drove home she began thinking about Alan, her beloved brother, and then wondered about his family. She had never liked his wife but he had had two sons who must both now be middle-aged. She really should try to get in touch with them after all these long years.

After she had put the car away, she thought it might be a good idea to ring Harrow and ask the Bursar if he knew where the family had moved to.

With the Bursar himself she drew a blank, but was told to hold the line as there was a master still at the school who might know.

It was a long wait while the man used another phone, but he came back with an answer. One of the sons was a master at Rugby – he could give her the number. She waited and after a while was given a Rugby school number.

She thanked the Bursar effusively and rang the number right away. It seemed she was speaking to one of the housemasters and when she mentioned her nephew's name he said at once that he could look up his number. Robert was the elder of the two sons she knew. It seemed he was a senior classics master and she wrote down the telephone number gratefully.

After a few minutes she dialled it and a diffident voice said, 'Robert Sankey speaking'.

He did not sound at all like his Father but she boldly said, 'You may not remember me at all. I am Jenny Lander, your aunt. I am so sorry I have not been in touch with you in all these long years but would very much like to meet you and your brother.'

'Well, hello, Aunt Jenny. Eric and I have often mentioned you but never done anything about contacting you. I should very much like to see you and I am sure my brother would too. Eric is teaching at that posh school Millfield but I can give you his number, or perhaps, better still, I will tell him you rang and next holidays perhaps we can meet.'

'How is your Mother?' Jenny asked.

'Oh, she died a few years after my Father. We all lived in London for a while until she died then we sold the house and each now have our own.'

'I would so like you both to come and visit me here near Beaconsfield. It's a big house and I can put you up. Perhaps we could make a date for you to come when the holidays start?'

'That sounds a good idea. Give me your address and number and I will have a word with Eric and then get back to you.'

Jenny did as he asked and, saying how very pleased she was to have found him, hung up.

So they were both academics like her much-loved brother. She hadn't asked if they were married and had children. That could all be established later. The best thing was to see her brother's sons first. She felt quite elated.

There was really no need for her ever to feel lonely while members of her family were to be contacted. She must entertain more – widen her circle of friends, otherwise when Mandis left school and got started on his career she would be very lonely.

She was pleased when Robert rang her one evening a few days after they had spoken. He had been in touch with Eric and, as they both had a mid-term exeat in two weeks' time, they would be pleased to accept her invitation and come to see her arriving for lunch on Saturday and leaving on Sunday afternoon. They would arrive from different directions but together as they had agreed to rendezvous in Reading at eleven o'clock.

She went to warn Didier about all the meals he would have to prepare but he seemed quite undaunted, and said he hoped Mandis would be able to come over to meet his cousins for lunch on the Sunday.

How wonderful it would be if he had done well in his finals. She would be so proud to introduce him to his much older and obviously intellectual cousins.

She knew that any day now Mandis would be ringing her with his results and kept herself busy planning menus for that particular weekend.

She prepared two of the guest rooms too, making up the beds and choosing suitable coloured towel sets, soap and so on for the bathrooms.

Not wanting to leave the house in case Mandis phoned, she invited Lulu and Filly over for pre-lunch drinks one morning. Lulu was looking much older and had taken to wearing rather masculine clothes and high leather boots which Jenny did not care for, but Filly, on the other hand, pregnant with her first baby, was blooming and very happy.

Lulu asked for her usual vodka tonic but Filly would only drink orange juice. In the midst of their talk of Lulu's unhappy marriage and Filly's happy one, the telephone rang and, picking it up, Jenny heard Mandis on the line. He sounded odd, unhappy. She excused herself and said she would take the call elsewhere, and raced upstairs as fast as she could.

'Mandis?' she panted.

'Yes,' came a voice she hardly recognised, 'it's your no-good son. I failed.'

She gasped not knowing what to say when there was a wild shriek at the other end and Mandis's normal voice saying, 'I really had you fooled, didn't I? Ya-hoo – I passed the lot with honours. I can now be commissioned as a sub-lieutenant or go on to Dartmouth!'

'Oh, my darling, don't do such things to me. Congratulations, my love, I always knew you would make it. When can you come home?'

'I have to wait for the official certificates, then I can have two days off. Will let you know – must rush now, lots of hugs and kisses.'

Jenny wandered slowly down the stairs with tears in her eyes and the two women stared at her.

Lulu said, 'Bad news?'

'No, I'm crying because I'm so happy. Mandis has passed all his exams with honours. He can be a fully fledged commissioned naval officer from now on – pour me one of your vodka tonics Lulu – we have to celebrate.'

She collapsed onto the settee and Lulu handed her her glass. They all said, 'Cheers' and drank and Jenny blew her nose and tried to pull herself together.

After her heart had stopped beating so wildly she explained how Mandis had first tricked her then told her the truth. They knew the boy and his sense of humour and laughed with her.

She tried to persuade them to stay to lunch but they both had men waiting for them at home and hurried away.

She went to the kitchen with a tray of dirty glasses and told Didier the marvellous news and he shook her hand and then kissed it, saying how pleased he was for his friend Mandis.

At least she would have some news with which to regale her guests at their forthcoming visits, the family on Sunday and her nephews the following weekend.

'Sit down and I will make you a superb omelette, madame,' Didier begged and she did as he suggested. They had a nice peaceful lunch together, and then some excellent coffee.

In bed that night Jenny thought hard and long about what Mandis would really like to do. She would gladly send him to Dartmouth and he could prepare for the Royal Navy, or if he really wanted to work in the Merchant Service, he could get started right away. She lay awake a long time pondering all this and then fell into a troubled sleep in which she saw herself discussing the subject with Myles. He, of course, would settle for nothing less than Dartmouth.

She woke up at four and went to the window. It was barely light but the birds were waking up and twittering in the trees. She wished she had someone close with whom she could discuss the matter. She might get a chance of a few minutes alone with Jonathan on Sunday, but it was unlikely with his wife and children around.

Children! Tim was now working with the now famous designer Conran and Fleur had been accepted at RADA. They both still lived at home but would be setting up their own pads any time now. They were not very interested in her adopted son, although they both seemed to like his company.

She need not have worried. The family arrived on time in Jonna's car and Didier surpassed himself and made a memorable lunch. He gave them the most wonderful onion soup with the floating brown bread, a whole filet of beef en croute with baby cauliflowers and pommes sautés such as they had never tasted before, and to follow, a huge perfectly turned out crème caramel with fresh cream. Excellent coffee as always, and Jonna asked permission to go to the cellar for a bottle of old brandy. Jenny had forgotten what the cellars contained, but Jonna told her she had a small gold mine down there.

While the rest of the family lay about in the drawing room reading the Sunday papers, Jenny asked Jonna to stroll round the garden with her and told him about Mandis and his success. Jonna seemed very pleased and advised her to let the boy choose his future for himself.

He was obviously intelligent and also longed to get to sea. The Merchant Navy might be right for him.

She thanked Jonna for his advice and he, putting a loving arm round her waist, thanked her for a superb lunch.

When they returned to the others they all got up saying they had things to do in the evening and must start back to town. Gayle was the only one who didn't enthuse about the meal or kiss her goodbye, but they had never liked each other and Jenny had long since accepted the fact.

She asked Tim about his new job and he said it was great and that one of his designs had been accepted for the new collection. He would let her know when the garment was to be shown.

She asked him if he had a girlfriend.

He replied, 'Several, if you must know, just playing for the time being.'

She was glad when they all finally left and hurried indoors to find that Didier had cleared most of the debris in the dining room, and she was only able to load the dish washer. He was a sweet, good-tempered man and a truly magnificent cook. She would be really sad to see him go, but he deserved to rise to greater things and now he had some English he was keen to start his hotel training.

Mandis rang again the next day and said he was not allowed to leave until term ended. He had been severely reprimanded for his last trip home and he dare not risk any more black marks. When he did come home he would be bringing his certificates.

TWENTY-TWO

The weekend visit of her nephews turned out to be an absolute disaster. They arrived in separate shabby old cars and looked like elderly twins. Portly, in good but shabby suits, they both wore thick-lensed glasses.

They had not the slightest likeness to her beloved brother. They were impressed by the house and by their luxurious rooms and went into rhapsodies over Didier's cooking. They talked about schools and politics and ecology in high-flown phrases, most of which went right over Jenny's head, but they ate like refugees and had second helpings of everything.

Jenny ventured to ask if they were married. Robert was, and had two small girls, but Eric was a bachelor. She decided after their first meal together that it would be their last and she had no wish to meet the rest of Robert's family.

They took walks round the garden, lingered in the Orangerie and spent hours perusing Myles' book collection.

Time dragged and, after listening to a lot of Mozart, some Vivaldi and quite a lot of Wagner, the long drawn-out meals were a blessing. Jenny did all the fetching and carrying between dining room and kitchen, but kind Didier insisted on clearing up.

At long last it was time for them to leave. She watched them get into their second-hand cars and waved them goodbye with enormous relief. It had not been a good idea. It would certainly not be repeated. Perhaps an exchange of Christmas cards, she thought, and thinking again, scratched their names out of her Christmas card book. Mandis would certainly not understand them.

She really must remember to ask Jonna what had happened to Myles' flat in the Albany. If Mandis was shortly to be going up to the city for interviews, he might like to use it. She rang Jonna at his office and he

136

explained that the flat had been let on a long lease to a young lawyer of whom Myles would have approved. He would keep an eye on it and if she wanted to do something different at the end of the present lease she should feel free to let him know.

Didier asked her diffidently if he might invite his sister over to stay one weekend. She replied that she would be very pleased to meet her and she should stay as long as she liked.

The girl arrived the weekend Mandis came home and he was as enchanted as she herself was by the pretty eighteen-year-old. Her name was Sophie, she was a natural blonde with a makeup-free, heart-shaped face with wide grey eyes. She was apprenticed to a couturier as Jenny herself had wanted to do in her teens, and this formed a bond between them instantly.

She spoke very little English so the weekend inevitably turned into a French one. They all ate in the kitchen and Jenny could see that Mandis was very drawn to the lovely girl.

Sophie made him promise that after he started work, he would spend part of his first leave visiting her family. Mandis replied readily in passable French, then asked Jenny if he could take Sophie for a drive in her car. Jenny agreed gladly and the young pair went off in the direction of Henley. She had promised Mandis a car of his own but it seemed wiser now to wait until he had settled in a job and got his first leave. She hoped he wouldn't crave for a fast sports car.

They were all sad to see Sophie leave. Mandis drove her to Heathrow and when he came back told his Mother how very much he liked the girl.

For the following days Jenny insisted, for Didier's sake, that they should all speak French for very soon he was to leave too, and she reckoned he had improved his English vocabulary well enough to start his course in Geneva.

It was a sad parting. Didier was surprised that she was not going to engage another cook but do the work herself. Jenny explained that, with the help of Mrs Blick, who now came in for several hours every day, she would be happy to try out all the fine dishes Didier had taught her. She wished him all the luck in the world and gave him an extra hundred pounds as a leaving present.

Mandis drove the Frenchman and his baggage to the airport and Jenny had an excellent lunch ready for Mandis when he returned.

The next morning's post brought a letter from a merchant shipping company operating in the City. This no doubt was instigated by Pangbourne College and Mandis received it with enthusiasm.

Jenny drove him to catch a train from Reading and begged him not to commit himself to anything without first consulting her. She would have liked to have driven him up to town herself but hated driving in the City and anyway, it was high time the boy began to find his own way about.

She felt very much on edge all day until he telephoned about five and asked her to pick him up at Reading Station an hour or so later.

On the way home he gave her a blow-by-blow account of the interview and said he had in fact been offered a job which would entail a short training period at Portsmouth and, if all went well, he would be taken on as a sub-lieutenant on a cargo ship.

'It sounds reasonable, darling. You must think about it carefully before you make a final decision.'

'Oh, I think I have more or less made up my mind. I want to go to sea and the sooner the better!' he said heartily.

'When do you have to give your answer?'

'Tomorrow.'

'Well, sleep on it,' she advised.

He drove expertly by now, if a little on the fast side, and she told him he should choose his own car on his first leave.

He was delighted to hear this and as soon as they were back at Foresters, he slung his bag on the doorstep, helped her out and drove the car to the garage. When he got back to join her she had poured him a shandy and mixed herself a vodka tonic. They drank to his new job and then went to the kitchen where she prepared him a Didier-style omelette with lots of asparagus and a bottle of Blanc de Blanc.

Relaxing in the drawing room after their meal he told her he intended to write his acceptance the very next day. He told her he was really keen to get to sea and, glancing across at him and seeing those strange eyes, she thought how proud Spiros would have been of him.

The next morning's post brought two letters from Sophie. One for each of them. To Jenny the young French girl had thanked her charmingly for her hospitality and said she hoped their two families would keep in touch.

Mandis read out bits of his letter. Sophie invited him to visit her during his first leave from his job and exclaimed how lovely his mother was. *'Elle est si belle, jeune et elancée, et elle a les yeux fantastique . . .'* the girl had written. Mandis had gone quite pink while reading out these bits and it was obvious to Jenny that Mandis was very smitten with her.

Jenny left Mandis in peace in Myles' study to write his letter to the shipping company and fill in various forms the next morning. When he had finished, she walked with him to the post and they dropped it into the pillar-box together.

In the afternoon they went over to Wycombe to see a film Jenny had seen well reviewed and had an early dinner at a nearby pub.

In bed that night Jenny began to dread the thought of Mandis leaving her. At first it would only be for a short training period, but she had to face the fact that soon it would be for good.

They had both been invited to a cocktail party at Lulu's the following evening. Jenny spent most of the day sorting through her wardrobes to find something suitable to wear and settled on a grey-blue silk cat-suit with a long matching stole. She tried it on and paraded up and down for Mandis's approval.

'Smashing!' he said. 'It's time you got yourself a man. You ought to get married again – of course I would have to approve of the guy. But I can't bear the thought of leaving you all alone in this vast house.'

There were a lot of people at Lulu's party and several spare men. One in particular she liked because he had a look of her dear brother Alan, but she did nothing to encourage the man. They left the party early and went home.

Mandis helped her to make dinner. He watched fascinated while she made *croques messieurs*, a dish which Didier had taught her and which consisted of French toast rolled round fried bacon and melted cheese. They ate several and then ice cream from the freezer.

Mandis made the coffee. There was a late telephone call from a rather drunken Lulu asking if she may give Jenny's number to the man who looked like Alan.

Jenny said, 'All right, but not for a while.'

Mandis said she must not play so cold and hard to get. She really needed friends and certainly the company of a man from time to time.

What did he know about life? How could he be suddenly so wise, so caring? It was enough that he loved her. She would always be a part of his life. What he could never know was her unforgettable experience with his Father. How could she ever tell him it was because of his Father that she loved him so much more than her own natural son?

It was possible she could strike up a relationship with another man; like the man who had looked a little like Alan at Lulu's party. He was a doctor, a specialist, her friend had told her later, and a widower. But she could never marry again. Another marriage was out of the question. Yet she had this great big house which she loved, so much money and there was so much life left over to kill.

She walked all round the place, touching much-loved objects here and there. She wandered into the Orangerie, which was now a mass of priceless plants, some bearing flowers, others fruit. It needed people to admire, to enjoy it. She thought of Myles and his first wonderful declaration of love for her. She thought of his rapid deterioration and his bloody terrifying death. She thought of Jonna's birth and his babyish ways, frowned on by his strict Father, and laughed. She had loved him until the American girl had taken him away from her. He had changed after he married but there was a lot of him in her grandson Tim. She must see more of him. She prayed he would find a wife who understood him and loved him for his gentleness as she did.

Mandis would fall in love – perhaps he had already with the French girl Sophie. He would have children. She would love them. The old house would come alive again with childish cries and laughter.

After Mandis had gone away, she would get a voluntary job in a local hospital – perhaps pushing a trolley of books round for the bed-ridden, or being a receptionist during difficult hours. There were many, many things she could do.

She noticed that it had begun to rain quite heavily. She stood in the drawing room, her face against one of the silken expensive curtains, trying to pin down her predicament. The rain fell softly and steadily as if it would go on for ever. She thought of Spiros' face, the feel and the smell of him. Never to her dying day could she ever forget him. The thought of another marriage was totally repugnant. She shuddered.

She looked out across the wet lawn. There was a movement, a small greyish animal was crawling towards her. It was dragging a hind leg. Was it a rabbit, a squirrel? No, it was a greyish tabby half-grown cat but it was badly injured, probably in pain. She hurried to the kitchen and grabbed a towel and rushed out by the back door. Rounding the house she stopped then began to move very slowly towards it. Regardless of the soaking rain she moved cautiously towards the small animal. It was a long haired greyish tabby, its fur flattened by the rain, its bright golden eyes pleading.

She kneeled and covered it gently with the towel and scooped it up. The body was tiny and thin. As she held it in the crook of her arm it looked up into her face and gave a silent miaow.

Hurrying now she went back into the house and placed it gently on the soft sofa cushion. It lay still. Perhaps it was dying. Probably run over. She knew the vet's number by heart. He was in at his surgery and available. She said urgently she would be over in a few minutes.

Dragging her old Burberry from the hall cupboard she pulled it on, picked up her bag with all her keys inside and, carefully lifting the small animal, hurried out to her car.

She laid the little animal on a rug on the front seat, started the engine and turned into the drive.

She realised that she was holding her breath, then, with the utmost care not to jolt the injured animal, began to breathe normally and headed for the vet's house.

He was a nice middle aged man who had been many times to Foresters when Ben and Ming were alive.

'What have we here?' he asked.

'It's a small cat – its one back leg seems crushed – it must have been run over.'

He put on his strong overhead light and placed the kitten on the table. Slowly he began feeling it gently all over with his skilled fingers. Then he concentrated on the limp back leg.

For minutes he said nothing, then, looking up at her said, 'The bone is not broken, just very badly bruised.' He began to massage the clotted fur gently and the little cat made another silent miaow and Jenny could see its exquisite pink tongue and mouth.

'All this little chap, sorry girl, needs is a bit of loving care,' the vet said, and Jenny felt the pain in her insides cease.

'Keep her warm and quiet. Give her a saucer of warm milk and you'll soon have her sharpening her claws on your best furniture,' he said.

'Thank you so very much. I am so relieved,' Jenny told him. 'Please send me your bill as usual.'

'No bill,' the vet said. 'You are obviously going to keep her; there will be bills to come, no doubt. Goodbye and drive carefully.'

The little cat was going to be all right. Of course she would keep her. On her way back to the house she prayed to God out loud, 'Thank you God for saving this small animal, and thank you for my health and strength.'

After all, being well was all that mattered.

TWENTY-THREE

To her surprise, the Siamese T'ang, now her pet for some considerable time after the death of Ming, accepted the new kitten and Jenny was delighted by this. She was even more surprised to see the vet drive up early one evening a few days later.

She walked out to meet him and he explained that, as he was passing on his way home, he thought he would look in and see how the injured kitten was faring. T'ang miaowed a loud greeting and the kitten, who had not yet been named, gave a silent 'Miaow'.

Declan Blunt picked the little scrap up gently and felt its hind leg carefully. For the first time Jenny noticed what beautiful hands he had.

As he stroked the kitten she found herself putting her own right hand on top of his. Immediately she felt foolish and he looked up into her eyes. His were grey with darker flecks in the iris. He had flushed slightly and, putting the kitten back into its basket, straightened up and turned to her.

'Actually, I have to confess that it wasn't the kitten I came to see. It was you. I thought of you all alone in this great house and, after your visit the other day, I couldn't get you out of my mind . . .'

It was Jenny's turn to blush now and, as she did so, took his arm and led him into the drawing room.

'This calls for a drink,' she said firmly, and hurried away to fill the ice-bucket.

They had several drinks, sitting side by side on the big sofa, and he agreed to stay for a cold supper. She found herself animating herself as she had not done for a very long time. She knew that he had been a widower for many years and had no children. She had always liked him but never considered him more than just 'the vet'. When he left after several hours of delightful conversation, he kissed her gently on her cheek

143

and asked if he may look in again soon.

'I would like nothing better – whenever you like,' she replied.

The following morning he telephoned to thank her and she asked if he was free for dinner. 'This time I will cook something special for you,' she added, and was happy to hear him accept.

She prepared a dish she had learned from Didier: *poulet au citron* with long grained rice.

Leaving it in a very low oven she went upstairs for a long luxurious bath and some serious thinking. She knew Declan was much older than herself; it would be almost like being with Myles again. So what? He would be a wonderful companion. The house would come alive again. He had a pair of very well-behaved Dalmatian dogs. Would they savage the cats?

They spent many evenings together and she grew as fond of him as he seemed to be of her.

A month later he asked her to marry him. She accepted. He gave up his clinic saying it was high time he retired, sold his house and the practice, and moved into Foresters. Jenny installed him in Myles's old suite. The well-behaved dogs seemed to come alive again.

Jenny and Declan were married in a register office with Jonathan and Lulu as witnesses. With their affectionate cats and dogs, life was full of laughter. The bedraggled tabby kitten grew into a big friendly cat whom they christened Cupid.

Declan took over the care of the Orangerie and, although they lived a celibate life, they laughed a lot and Jenny, with the homecoming of Mandis to look forward to, felt happier than she had ever been in her life.